LONE WOLFE PROTECTOR

A WOLFE CREEK SERIES NOVEL

KAYLIE NEWELL

Entangled Publishing, LLC
2614 South Timberline Road
Suite 109
Fort Collins, CO 80525
Visit our website at www.entangledpublishing.com.

Covet is an imprint of Entangled Publishing, LLC.

Edited by Candace Havens and Allison Collins
Cover design by Curtis Svehlak

Manufactured in the United States of America

First Edition August 2014

For my parents.

Chapter One

The only thing that mattered now, was answers.

The mountains outside the little car passed in a blur. The leafy patches of autumn color were lovely, although subdued, in the early evening mist. Winter would soon follow, and no way did she want to be trapped in the mountains. Maggie Sullivan turned the knob on the radio, careful not to stop on anything too sad or too happy or too anything for that matter. Sometime during the last year, she had settled into a comfortable state of numb. Every other emotion she'd chosen not to work through, including anger and pain, would just have to wait.

She shifted and adjusted the seat belt over her shoulder, doing her best not to catch her reflection in the rearview mirror. She wasn't someone she liked to look at anymore. Her green eyes had taken on a hollow appearance, the circles underneath them, purple and bruised-looking. She had let her curls go back to their natural state of brown. Highlighting would require caring about something as trivial as hair color, and she wasn't fooling herself about that one anymore.

She cracked the window to get some fresh air and the smell of pine and wood smoke immediately invaded the car. Her stomach lurched and she rolled it back up again. She hated the smell of both.

Unwrapping a piece of bubble gum, she put it in her mouth, staring at the road ahead. *Aimee would tell me to take a chill pill. Chillax, girlfriend, she would have said.* It had been a year since she'd heard Aimee's voice. So long. Too long.

It was one of the things Maggie missed the most.

I'll be right back. The very last thing Aimee'd said.

Maggie's phone chimed from the passenger seat, and she jumped.

She glanced at it—yet another text from her mother, the third in an hour. This one was simple and to the point. *Please don't do this.* Maggie could almost hear the pleading words uttered in her mother's fading Irish accent. Nobody wanted this, least of all her parents. She knew they wondered if she was unbalanced or too full of grief to act rationally. The truth was, she wondered, too. But not going wasn't an option anymore. She simply couldn't stay put.

Shivering, she reached over to turn on the heater. When she looked up, the sign for Wolfe Creek loomed in the distance.

Tiny at first. Green and insignificant. Sitting at the edge of the dark forest, thick with trees and shrubbery. An ordinary person would have passed by without giving it a second thought. They would have driven along, too caught up in their kids' fighting or trying to decipher their GPS, to notice much.

But as the sign, and the town, got bigger and bigger, her heart became a scared, hunted thing inside her chest. She stared with eyes that stung from lack of moisture. Her hands tightened around the steering wheel as the smell of pine and wood smoke permeated the cab. It no longer mattered whether the windows were open or closed.

She took deep, even breaths, forcing herself to relax. How in God's name would she accomplish what she needed to if she couldn't even drive into town without passing out?

Easing the car off the freeway, she slowed to a stop in front of another sign, this one large and brown, and boasting of Wolfe Creek's historical status. She flipped the blinker on for absolutely no one's benefit, and turned left onto the deserted, bumpy road that led into town.

The seat belt dug into her neck, and she gave it an impatient tug. The mist had turned to fog, cold and ominous, and forcing her to the shoulder in order to see better.

This was it. This was the place she had visited in her nightmares too many times to count. She'd memorized every detail. The mechanic's shop with rusted-out beauties from the fifties out front. The post office, city hall, and general store, all ancient white buildings with burnished brass plaques mounted next to their front doors. She'd memorized every face she had seen that night, their expressions wary and a little resentful of outsiders. But she hadn't been back.

Until now.

"Can I help you?"

Maggie plopped the last suitcase down on top of the

other two and straightened to look across the counter into a kind, round face.

"Maggie Sullivan," she said, careful to stay aloof. She didn't trust anyone in Wolfe Creek, no matter how friendly they looked. "I have a reservation."

"Oh, yes." The woman flipped through a worn ledger. "Here you are. Our guest who's staying—"

"Indefinitely," Maggie said, cutting her off.

The woman, Ara, judging by her name tag, continued undeterred. "We're happy to have you, honey." Her curly brown hair was threaded with gray. Her large breasts and plump waist met somewhere in the middle underneath a soft, denim jumper. Grandmotherly. That's the word that came to Maggie's mind.

"You'll unfortunately have to share the main bath, which is down the hall from your room. Is that okay? It's stocked with plenty of essentials, towels, shampoo and whatnot."

Maggie signed the debit-card receipt without looking up. "Share with whom?"

"Other guests. And we have a couple of boarders like you, staying on for the next few months."

"Perfect," she said, leaning down to pick up the suitcase.

"Your room is upstairs. Second on the left. Jim will carry in the rest of your bags. Just holler if you need anything, okay?"

"Thank you." Without looking back, Maggie trudged up the spiraling staircase, glancing at the black-and-white photographs on the way up.

The place was old. Actually, old was an understatement. From what Maggie had found on the internet, she knew The Wolfe Creek Inn had been built in 1883, and had been a working hotel for most of a century. The interior, although it had no doubt seen face-lifts throughout the decades, probably looked much like it had when it first opened. The furnishings were old fashioned, but in good shape; red velvet couches, heavy draperies with gold embroidery, and huge oriental rugs with elaborate designs woven throughout. The hotel was beautiful. Authentic. It even smelled old, in that pleasant, antique-y kind of way.

Hauling the suitcase up another step, Maggie examined the photographs to her left a little closer. Like the hotel itself, they were ancient. Most were pictures of people in turn of the century clothing. Women in long dresses and high, lacy collars. Men in dark suits with beat-up hats pushed high on their foreheads.

But some were less ordinary. And those were the ones that made her balance the suitcase on the step below and lean in to get a better look. Native Americans. Women in elaborate animal-skin wraps, men with feathers hanging from thick braids, half-naked children staring at the camera, wise beyond their years. Maggie looked up at a larger photo in a tarnished silver frame. In it was a young Indian woman wearing a beaded dress. At her side was a handsome white man in an equally fancy suit. His eyes were pale and came across as almost white in the colorless picture. It was obviously a wedding portrait.

And something about it gave her the chills.

"Like what you see?"

Startled, Maggie turned. A tall man stood at the top of the stairs watching her. He leaned casually against the wall with his hands in his pockets. Her first reaction was of stunned silence. Native American, and beautiful, if that was the right word. Smooth, olive skin. Shoulder-length black hair that caught the fading light of day through the window behind him. His cheekbones were high and pronounced, his eyes, dark and cutting.

She stood there with her mouth open, before remembering to snap it shut again. She didn't trust men. And certainly not any men in this Podunk town.

"Excuse me?"

He smiled, an unmistakable arrogance gracing his wide mouth. "Those are my great-great grandparents you're looking at. Good ol' Gran and Gramps."

"So?"

"So, you just looked curious, that's all." He took a step down, hands still in his pockets. "I could answer any questions you might have. Any at all."

"No, thanks." *You could always ask him where he was that night a year ago, Maggie.*

He continued down the steps, an odd mixture of grace and masculinity. When he brushed by, she caught the scent of the woods, cologne, tobacco, and something else she couldn't quite place, but that made her entire body tense just the same.

"You let me know if you change your mind," he said. "I'm in and out of here quite a bit."

"I'll do that," Maggie said grabbing her suitcase. She climbed a few steps before turning around, but he was already gone. Apparently he was not only exceptionally good-looking, but also very quick. She wouldn't have been able to make it down the stairs in half that time. But then again, he wasn't hauling half his closet in a box, either. She narrowed her eyes toward the bottom of the staircase where he should have been, before turning around to head to her room.

Maggie didn't sleep well, but that was nothing new. Bad dreams plagued her all night long, but when she woke to the precarious light of dawn, she couldn't remember any of them. They'd vanished like mist over a lake, only their disturbing effects lingering.

She sat up in bed and looked around. The room, like the rest of the Inn, was old fashioned. An antique mirror hung above the dark wood dresser, and several photographs of the hotel itself graced the walls that were painted a cheerful butter yellow. It was chilly, despite the elderly furnace's efforts to warm the place up. It creaked and popped in the corner as Maggie pulled the white eyelet bedspread up to her chest.

Today was the day. She took a deep breath and exhaled slowly. Now that she was here, she wasn't entirely convinced she'd made the right decision. But there was no turning back now. She had no idea where to start, but she wasn't going to leave this place without some answers. She needed them. To move on. To let go.

Throwing back the covers, she hopped across the frigid hardwood floor to her suitcases. Later today, she'd unpack. Get relatively comfortable in the room. But for now, she just wanted a hot shower and a cup of coffee. Grabbing a sweatshirt and some jeans, she made a beeline to the bathroom down the hall. Not in the mood to meet any other guests or compete for bathroom time for that matter, she was relieved when she didn't come across anyone else. She showered and dressed quickly, not bothering to dry her hair, and headed downstairs.

A chipper Ara stood behind the counter again. Honestly, everything about this woman seemed genuine. Not that it mattered to Maggie, of course.

"Good morning. Did you sleep well?"

"Okay," Maggie said. "But I usually don't sleep great wherever I am." She shrugged, eager to change the subject. "Do you have any recommendations for breakfast?"

"The Arrowhead Café is very good. They serve comfort food and the likes."

"Where is it?"

"Back down that way about a block and a half. You can't miss it. Big sign. Lots of pickup trucks out front."

Lots of pickup trucks. Could this place get any more *Deliverance*?

Ara eyed Maggie's wet hair. "You'll need a jacket, honey. It's cold out."

"I'm okay, thanks." Maggie walked out, catching the screen door before it slammed.

Gritting her teeth, she dug her hands into her jean pockets. *Crap.* It *was* cold. But she'd rather sit on hot coals than go back and get a jacket, or admit she was wrong to anyone. Even sweet Ara, whom she'd really wanted to hug this morning, in spite of herself.

She walked down the side of the road with her chin tucked into her chest. Her damp curls lay against the back of her neck like a wet blanket, and she had to work to keep her teeth from chattering. A pile of leaves burned nearby, and the smoke stung the inside of her nose.

Making her way to the café, she kicked up clouds of dirt

with her sneakers, and wondered what Aimee would have thought about all this. She had a pretty good idea. She'd think Maggie was nuts, just like everyone else. Who else would quit their job and take every penny of their savings to embark on a wild goose chase that had a very good chance of ending no better than it began? *Margaret Sullivan, that's who.* Maggie imagined her mother spouting off this last sentence in her most jaunty St. Paddy's Day voice.

Looking up, Maggie studied the mostly deserted main road through town. It was still fairly early, but shouldn't there be people out walking? Driving to work? Her footsteps punctuated the strange silence, but did nothing to ease the chills that had popped up along her arms. In fact, her skin prickled everywhere and she shuddered. Slowing, she looked over her shoulder. *Nobody.*

But the sudden feeling of someone watching had taken hold. The fact that she couldn't see anyone didn't matter. She *felt* them. She glanced at the shrubbery to her left, which as far as she could tell, led straight into the forest. It was dark and wet, with drops of condensation spattering steadily on the blanket of dead leaves below.

"Hello?"

Her voice didn't sound like her own. Anxiety laced it like poison. It was hard to believe there'd actually been a time when she hadn't been scared of her own shadow. But things had changed a year ago. She'd changed.

She stood there a second longer, staring into the bushes as if they were going to come alive or reveal a secret only she would be privy to. Still nothing.

Taking a small step away, and then another, she had to resist the urge to turn and break into a run.

When Maggie finally got to the café, three blocks over, her heart had slowed to a normal rhythm again. Looking around, she made a mental note that Ara seemed to be right about a lot of things. The temperature being only one. The parking lot was full of trucks; four-by-fours, twin cabs, lifted, lowered, you name it. The only thing they all had in common was a thick layer of mud coating their oversize tires. And over the mud, a layer of dust, as if the hillbilly fairies had sprinkled it there in afterthought.

So this is where everyone is. Apparently breakfast was an important social event in Wolfe Creek. Bracing herself, Maggie walked in the front door.

Every soul in the café stopped and looked up. After a few uncomfortable seconds, a pretty waitress smiled and gestured toward a table in the corner. "Have a seat."

Maggie made her way across the room, doing her best to ignore the stares that followed.

She sat and scooted the chair up to the table, where a dog-eared paper menu lay open as if waiting for her to arrive.

"Hi there."

Looking up, Maggie realized she'd been wrong. The waitress wasn't pretty. She was absolutely stunning. Her uniform screamed early eighties with its pink collar and matching apron. Ample breasts pushed at the fabric, the buttons looking strained from the considerable duty of holding them in. She wore several gold chains, heavy dangly earrings, and a generous amount of makeup. Her short, strawberry-blond hair was teased and sprayed, and looked more like a wig than anything else.

"I'll be your server this morning, hon. My name's Candi. Can I get you started with some coffee?"

"Please."

"Coming right up."

She walked behind the counter, hips swinging like the pendulum on a grandfather clock. Maggie had always been slender, boyish, and she crossed her arms over her chest self-consciously.

When Candi came back, she set the coffee down, leaned against the table, and eyed Maggie through blue-tinted mascara. "Don't think I've seen you around before. Just passing through?"

Maggie took a sip and burned her tongue. Swearing inwardly, she set the coffee back down and wondered how much she should reveal about her stay in Wolfe Creek right off the bat. This was a small town. People would talk when they found out who she was and why she was here. But they'd find out soon enough, anyway.

"Nope. I'll be here a while."

"Where are you staying?"

Maggie looked up and saw Candi's cheerful smile. Probably just curious, like most people in a town this size would be. If Maggie wanted answers, she was going to have to talk. Ask questions. Gain some trust. Maybe Candi would be a good place to start. "The Wolfe Creek Inn."

"Ah," she said. "Where are you from?"

Suddenly cold, Maggie wrapped her hands around the steaming cup of coffee. "Seattle, originally. My family moved to Portland when I was two."

"Have you ever been to our neck of the woods before?"

Maggie's throat constricted like it always did when she thought of her one and only visit to Wolfe Creek. "I have. Last year, as a matter of fact."

"Last year?"

Maggie nodded.

"When last year?" If Candi meant to push, it wasn't obvious. She still wore an amiable expression that Maggie couldn't help but warm to.

"Last fall. October."

Candi's smile faded. And for the first time Maggie noticed the fine lines around her green eyes. "When last October?"

"Right before Halloween. October thirtieth."

Candi didn't say a word. Instant recognition lit her face. She knew who Maggie was.

And her reason for being in town.

Chapter Two

"I'd love to ask you a few questions, if I could," Maggie said, worried that Candi would simply turn her back and walk away. Tip be damned.

"I'm so sorry for what happened, hon. I really am. But we've all told the police everything we know."

Maggie smiled nervously. "Well, I'm not the police, so…"

"I know you're not." Candi threw a look over her shoulder, then leaned close to the table. "I understand you want to find out for yourself. Hell, I'd probably do the same if I were you. I've seen you on the news. I know how much you want to find your friend. But this isn't the kind of town an outsider goes snooping around in."

Before Candi could move away, Maggie grabbed her hand. It was an uncharacteristic move. In the last year, she'd grown introverted and distrustful. She didn't like to touch people, and she didn't like to be touched. But deep down, she felt like this girl might be able to help. And that was worth reaching out for.

"Please," she said, surprised at the desperation in her voice. "I don't know where to start."

Candi considered this. "I know." She took a breath and glanced over her shoulder again. "I'll tell you one thing," she whispered, "you can't just go around asking a bunch of random people questions. If you're going to find anything out, and I really don't know *if* there's anything to find out, but if there is, you'll have to start at the top. Work your way to the bottom. Do you understand what I'm saying?"

Maggie shook her head, feeling thick.

"The sheriff's department."

Maggie knew who the sheriff of Deep Water County was. She'd seen him on the news, read about him in the paper, called him too many times to count, only to be brushed off, as usual. "I've tried," she said. "He won't talk to me."

"I'm talking about the deputies. The sheriff won't talk to you, but I'm betting a few of the deputies would."

"Who? Which ones?"

At that moment, the door to the café opened, bringing with it an icy gust of wind and a tall, broad-shouldered man in uniform.

Candi smiled. "That one, right there."

Maggie shifted in her chair, her shoulder blades biting into the rigid wood backing. The deputy looked down at her, openly hostile, his gaze dark and flat, his jaw tight.

"Maggie, this is Deputy Wolfe. Koda, this is Maggie," Candi said.

"Sullivan," Maggie finished, forcing a smile and sticking out her hand. "Maggie Sullivan."

He didn't take it. "I know who you are. What are you

doing here?"

It took a second for that to sink in. She couldn't shake the fact that he looked familiar. Native American, like so many other people in town. And gorgeous. *One thing about it,* she thought, *Wolfe Creek has good genes.* His jet-black hair, worn short and a little messy, made him look rugged, dangerous…and very attractive. He had a prominent jaw, a straight, narrow nose, and a wide mouth, set in an unfriendly line. His eyes, black as his hair, shone with an intensity that made her uncomfortable.

She took a sip of coffee and her hand shook. She set the cup down, hoping he hadn't noticed. Glancing up, she tried to ignore his incredibly inconvenient good looks and focus on what really mattered.

"I'm here to try and find out what happened to my friend. Is that okay with you?" *Ouch.* She immediately wished she could bite the words back. If she wanted answers, she'd have to make some friends. And this wasn't the way to do it. Hot Deputy-1. No Filter Maggie-0.

"No," he said. "It's not okay with me. The investigation is still ongoing, and we don't need any complications. That includes you." He said this last part while looking her up and down.

"Ha. Investigation? What investigation? As far as I can tell, no one has investigated anything for the last six months."

Candi slapped a hand on the table. "*Hush,* you two. You want the whole town to hear?" She looked at Maggie. "I can promise you, Deputy Wolfe wants to find your friend just as much as you do. And he's been working really, really hard to make that happen. And you," she said, turning to the man taller than her by at least a foot, "it wouldn't kill you to show some manners. I just got done telling Maggie here that you'd help."

"Well, I sure wish you hadn't," he said, his eyes still locked with Maggie's. Even more intimidating than the gun on his hip was the way he stood, his posture full of tension and unpredictability. Something about it reminded Maggie of a wild animal. Only his official tan, sheriff's department uniform made her feel somewhat safe in his presence. Otherwise, she wouldn't have gone near him with a ten-foot pole.

"I think someone in this town knows what happened to Aimee. With all due respect, Deputy, I'm not leaving Wolfe Creek until I find out who."

She expected a biting response, but after a few seconds he just shrugged. "It's a free country, sister." He nodded to Candi, turned his back, and headed to a booth on the other side of the café where a couple other men waited.

"Wow. Is he always like that?"

Shaking her head, Candi topped off Maggie's coffee. "He can be a little gruff. Koda's small town, through and through. But he's a good deputy. I can promise you that."

"Wait. Deputy *Wolfe*. As in Wolfe Creek?"

"One in the same. His ancestors settled here at the end of the 1800s. His great-great granddaddy married a Tututni Indian woman. They were the ones who built the Inn, where you're staying."

"Interesting," Maggie said, sneaking a look in his direction. He seemed to have dismissed her completely, talking in low tones to the men he sat with.

"It was a big scandal back then. You can imagine. A white man marrying outside his own race. But they were very much in love. Or so the story goes."

Maggie nodded and sipped her coffee. There seemed to be more to the little town of Wolfe Creek than she'd originally thought.

"Oh, my." Candi smiled and it lit up her entire face. Her earrings glittered against her neck and looked totally out of place next to the dowdiness of the café. "Here I am lecturing Koda about his manners, and I've gone and forgotten my own. It's nice to meet you." She extended a manicured hand.

"Nice to meet you, too." Maggie said.

And surprisingly enough, she meant it.

Koda Wolfe sat in his department issued SUV, a dusty, green-and-white Ford Explorer, with the engine running. A continuous cloud of exhaust rolled onto the night air, accompanied by the low, patient rumble of the motor.

The Inn sat across the street, its historical elegance in direct contrast to the town's one and only tavern, which sidled up right next to it. Bill's Tavern was where everyone and their dog got sauced on Saturday nights, and all the nights in between.

Every now and then, someone would go in or out, releasing a steady stream of bar smoke, music, and a "fuck you" or two.

Koda watched and waited, not quite apathetic, but close. He'd seen it all before, hundreds of times. Drinking, fights, jealousy over women. Plain boredom. Everything that accumulated over years of living in a town that was essentially cut off from the rest of the world. Mountain living was hard. And these people were harder. It took a special kind of person to be able to make it here, and he was constantly questioning his own motive for sticking around.

Blinking into the darkness, he looked back at the Inn and the small yellow car parked out front. It stuck out like a sore thumb, and something about that irritated him. *Maggie Sullivan.* He'd recognized her immediately this morning. She'd initially been a suspect in Aimee Styles's disappearance, just like everyone else in Wolfe Creek. But that had been standard procedure, and she'd been ruled out almost immediately.

For the better part of a year, she'd been on everything from CNN to *Good Morning America* trying to get the word out about her best friend, whose face haunted him nearly every night in his sleep. And in doing so, had made his life a living hell. Investigating a disappearance in a town this small, where everyone knew everyone else, and therefore, protected everyone else, was hard enough without some busybody city girl trying to play detective.

And now here she was. Different in many ways than she'd looked on TV, but her eyes were the same. Wide, green, and distrustful. Her creamy white skin had the look of someone who didn't get outside much. A small spattering of freckles across her nose, coupled with wild brown curls and a slender frame, made her look young, although he knew for a fact she was in her mid-twenties. No doubt she was pretty. Maybe even beautiful in a delicate kind of way. And that annoyed him.

When he walked into the café earlier this morning, he'd wanted to haul her up by those delicate shoulders, put her in her car, and send her packing. But what he'd said was true. It was a free country, and he had no control whether she stayed or went. What he *did* have control over, however, was how much he chose to acknowledge her visit. Ignoring her though, would be difficult to damn near impossible, if she befriended people like Candi, who, although well intentioned, had a mouth the size of a ten-gallon drum.

He caught sight of a shadowy male figure emerging from the side door of the Inn. He walked toward the truck, head down, shoulders hunched, with the half-moon overhead casting just enough light so that Koda could make out his long dark hair.

Rolling down the window, he waited as the man approached.

"Ahh, big brother. To what do I owe tonight's visit?"

"Just making sure you stay out of trouble," Koda said. "As usual."

Zane Wolfe leaned against the truck, his worn jean jacket sliding against the paint job and pulled out the butt-ugly gold-embossed lighter that he'd bought on his eighteenth birthday. Koda had the sudden urge to knock it out of his hand. Just like Zane to invest so much in something so bad for him.

Tapping out a cigarette, Zane lit it with practiced ease. It illuminated his darkly handsome face, before simmering to an understated orange glow.

"Don't you mean babysitting?"

"Whatever," Koda said.

"I'd call it infringing upon my civil rights. Shouldn't you be out fighting crime somewhere?"

"I'm stopping it before it starts."

"Now, that hurts. It really does. Are you implying I'm not a law-abiding citizen?"

"I'm implying that you've been in jail more times than

the average law-abiding citizen, yes. And what's with the scruff? Have you given up shaving altogether now?"

"I like it. Besides, it's coming in faster than I can shave it off."

"What's that? Once a week?"

Zane smiled at this and took a drag, his eyes narrowing through the blue smoke he exhaled. "Not to change the subject," he said. "But there's a young lady staying just down the hall from me. Goes by the name of Maggie Sullivan. *The* Maggie Sullivan. The one who believes her girlfriend is still out there, haunting the woods of Wolfe Creek or some such shit?"

Koda stiffened. "Zane—"

"She's not bad-looking. A little skinny for my taste, but I'm not above making an exception."

"Zane."

"What?"

"Stay away from her. Understand?"

"I'm just saying she has a nice ass, is all."

"Look all you want," Koda snapped. "But that's it."

Zane grinned, tilting his head in that cocky way that pissed Koda off so much, and had since the fifth grade. He flicked his cigarette into the frost-covered grass.

"Don't worry, brother. I'll keep my distance." Turning, he jammed his hands back in his pockets. "For now."

Before he could argue, Zane walked away, headed for the tavern, and probably a date with several tequila shots and a nasty hangover.

Koda watched him go, a familiar combination of love and fear in his heavy heart.

Chapter Three

Maggie had been watching the caretaker, Jim, through the sheer white curtains of her little room for the last half an hour. He was tall and gangly, and wore a dirty brown coat over jeans that were a shade dirtier. He'd been chopping and stacking wood, and something about the fluid way he moved, like it took no effort at all to raise the ax and slam it down again, made Maggie uneasy.

Pulling out a wire bound notebook, she took a steadying breath and scratched his name at the top. *Jim,* she wrote in bold, black letters. *Caretaker. Last name?*

She peeked back out the window, careful to stay behind the curtains. He stood below, ax poised in midair, his big feet planted wide. When he brought the blade down, splinters went flying and the sound of cracking wood reverberated through the still morning air. *Whack!*

Maggie flinched. His shoulders were thick, powerful. Despite his gray hair and scruff, she didn't think he was much older than fifty. Plenty of time to have a past.

After closing the notebook and stuffing it in her purse, Maggie stepped into her boots and pulled on her fleece jacket. She'd slept later than she'd wanted to, and was anxious to get outside. She'd explored a little yesterday, but had come back to the Inn when it started to rain. Discouraged, she'd sat up late, trying to decide what to do next. That's when she'd thought of keeping a log. People she'd met in Wolfe Creek, and people she hadn't yet. Names, dates, things that struck her as odd. All of it. Maybe she'd seen one too many episodes of *Murder, She Wrote,* but so be it. Whatever would lead to Aimee was exactly what she'd do.

She headed out the bedroom door, locked it behind her, and turned in a hurry to get outside.

"Whoa."

She jumped. It was the guy from yesterday, the one from the stairs. The fast one. The good-looking one. He was standing right behind her, and she hadn't heard a sound.

"In a rush?"

It took a second to recover. "Yes. No." She smoothed the front of her jacket as if it were a cocktail dress, and forced herself to look up at him. Definitely still good-looking. But something was different this morning. He was rough around the edges where he hadn't been yesterday. Dark smudges sat below his eyes and heavy stubble prickled his neck and jaw. His long hair hung next to his face, obscuring half of it in shadow.

"Which is it? Yes or no?"

"Yes. I'm in a hurry."

"Shame." He shook his head, never taking his black eyes off hers. "I was going to ask you to breakfast."

"Thanks, but no." The words tumbled out before she could help it. If she'd been thinking clearly, she would have accepted. There was no telling what this guy knew. He'd probably been around the block a few times. But there was something about him, something that made her want to shrink away. Maybe it was the way he looked. Maybe it was the way he smelled, like the forest itself, which she hated. Maybe it was both. But whatever it was, the thought of spending any length of time with him made her dizzy.

"Awfully quick to say no. You're going to ruin my reputation as a ladies' man."

"I'm not here to date." She walked around him. "Sorry about your reputation."

She was halfway down the hall before he spoke again. Quietly, as if in afterthought.

"I know why you're here."

She stopped and turned at the sound of his voice.

"You do?"

She was speaking to his back, his gray-flannel shirt doing nothing to hide its graceful curve, its long, lean muscle. "Of course. Everyone knows why you're here." Slowly he turned, and the arrogant smile was gone. "Only problem is, I'm sure you'll end up pointing your finger at someone innocent."

Her mouth hung open. She didn't know what she'd been expecting. But this wasn't it.

"This is a small town. We're small-town people. But that doesn't mean we're stupid. And it sure as hell doesn't mean we're killers."

He took a step toward her, and she shrank back.

"And I'll tell you another thing," he continued in a silky voice. "There are some people who might take exception to you pointing that pretty little finger of yours. They might not take it well at all."

Maggie stared at him, remembering Aimee, her sweet friend. And the fact that she'd probably never see her again. And just like that, her nerves vanished. In their place bubbled a white-hot anger.

"I don't care how they take it. I don't care how *you* take it. Something happened to her that night. She didn't just vanish into thin air. Someone did something to her."

They stood facing each other, silence settling eerily between them. The old hotel seemed to be listening. Or maybe its ghosts were listening. It felt like the place was full of them.

Whack! Another chop of wood from outside, and the spell broke. The full, pale lips stretched into a slow grin, and the handsome face transformed again, cocky, teasing.

"Just be careful," he said. "I'd hate to have anything happen to you before we can share that breakfast."

Before she knew how to respond, he turned and disappeared down the hall. After a second, she caught the faint sound of a door closing. Then the even fainter sound of a lock clicking behind it.

It was the one memory that kept coming back. The one that pushed itself ahead of all the others, the one that plagued her dreams, as well as her every waking moment.

It was the last half hour she'd spent with Aimee. In the cheerful yellow car, with the heater blasting, and classic rock thumping through the old, cracked speakers. Credence was going on about a bad moon, and Aimee was sitting with her boots kicked off, her long legs crossed on the seat like a kid's. Behind them, the night stretched beyond the car, into the forest and fog the consistency of cold pea soup.

They'd been laughing and talking. One of those long, emotional talks always so much better on a road trip, with bags of chips and candy bars between them. Aimee had said something that made Maggie turn, and that image was what stuck in her head. Aimee's dark silhouette against the foggy window, her face suddenly drawn and void of laughter.

"I had a terrible dream last night, Mags," she'd said.

"What kind of dream?"

She'd looked out the window and traced a small heart in the corner. "I was running from someone and I kept falling down." She'd turned back to Maggie. "You know those dreams where you're moving in slow motion? I was screaming for you. You were right behind me."

"I hate those." Despite the warmth of the car, Maggie had shivered. Aimee was usually sunny, upbeat. But when she had looked over, her blond hair soft against her face, Maggie frowned.

"Don't ever leave me, okay?" Aimee had said.

That had been almost a year ago. Maggie walked down the side of the road in Wolfe Creek, arms crossed over her chest, looking at the ground but not really seeing it. The last few months had been the worst of her life. As far as tragedy went, she had nothing to compare it to. She'd barely survived and felt lucky her mother hadn't simply committed her somewhere. She missed Aimee with a deep, painful ache that was always just beneath the surface. Guilt had plagued her for almost a year, now, so awful she had trouble sleeping most every night. *Don't leave me, okay?*

But she had left. She'd left, even though she hadn't wanted to. She'd left because the police had told her to. Because her family had wanted her home, safe. Because, even though the thought of leaving Wolfe Creek had been enough to make her want to shrivel up in the fetal position, she hadn't known what else to do.

So she'd come back. It had taken nearly a full year to save enough money. She'd quit her job as a copywriter, trying not to burn every bridge she had in the process, and convinced those around her that doing this would help her "heal" and find "closure." Whatever that meant.

But her parents had known the truth. She was going back to Wolfe Creek to try and find out what had happened. And she was planning on staying put as long as it took.

Every now and then, a truck passed, and the freezing air swooshing by nearly knocked her off-balance. But she kept walking, stubbornness and God knew what else, pushing her on.

Behind her, a car slowed and eased onto the gravel shoulder. A dirty red Grand Am sporting snow tires and a huge dent in the fender.

She eyed it warily.

The window cranked down and a head of teased hair poked out. "Hey!"

It was Candi, from the diner.

"Hey."

"Need a lift?"

Maggie studied the other woman for a long second, her bright red lips stretched into a smile, heavily made-up lashes blinking into the late-afternoon sun, gold necklaces glinting like pirate treasure around her neck. And suddenly, she just felt tired.

"Where are you headed?" Candi asked, shivering visibly through the open window.

"Um...I'm not really sure."

"It's too cold out here to be taking a walk, girl." They were scolding words, spoken in a bubble-gum tone. It was hard not to be drawn in by their kindness. In a way, Maggie wanted to be drawn in, if only to let go of some of the pain that hung like a lead weight around her heart. It was all so exhausting.

"Hop in." Candi nodded toward the passenger's seat. "I have a quick stop at the mechanic's, and then I'm gonna grab a cup of coffee before I head home." She took her hands off the wheel and rubbed them together briskly. "I'd love it if you joined me, Maggie. It's Maggie, right?"

Maggie nodded.

"What do you say?"

And just like that, Maggie's heart felt a fraction lighter. She hadn't grabbed a cup of coffee with anyone in over a year.

"Sure," she said, walking around to the passenger door. "Why not."

Chapter Four

The mechanic, Gary Pruit, lounged in his garage and watched them approach. He sat bathed in the fluorescent light of a single bulb that sprouted from the high, cobwebbed ceiling. It seemed to accentuate the dirt on his coveralls, as well as the stubble on his jaw.

Without taking his eyes off them, he turned to spit a brown stream of tobacco juice onto the floor.

"Candi," he said, nodding as politely as a man with a wad of chew in his mouth could manage, "what can I do for ya?"

Maggie stopped at the open door of the garage while Candi walked in, her tight black skirt riding up with each step she took. Gary didn't seem to notice, or if he did, was hiding it well. He kept looking from Candi to Maggie, and back again, as if they were going to steal something.

"Gary, you've got to fix that damn bumper. It keeps rubbing up against my front tire."

"Well, we can't have that, sugar." He smiled, residual

tobacco juice glistening on his lower lip. "I told you I could pop it out. But it's gonna run ya."

Candi dug a pack of gum from her purse. Popping a piece into her mouth, she grimaced.

"Yeah, I know," she said around the pink wad. "How *much* is it gonna run me?"

"Couldn't do it for less than three hundred."

"*What?* You know I can't afford three hundred."

"Might be closer to four."

"Shit."

"You can take it down the mountain. But there ain't no way they're fixing it for less, I guarantee you that." His gaze shifted toward Maggie, and he spit another brown stream. "But I'll tell you what."

Candi glanced back at her and rolled her eyes. "What," she said, facing Gary again.

"I'm having a poker game at my place next weekend. I'd do it for two, if you give us a private show."

Candi's curvaceous back straightened. "I don't do that anymore, Gary. You know that." Her voice dripped ice cubes. "Thanks for the offer, but I think I'll live with the damn dent."

Gary sneered at Maggie. As if she were the reason Candi had stopped doing whatever it was she used to do. "Who's this?"

"This is Maggie. She's from Portland. Maggie, this is Gary Pruit, the *only* mechanic in town."

Maggie nodded. "Nice to meet you." She didn't think she'd ever spoken such an outright lie. The guy made her want to bathe in lye soap, and made her more uncomfortable by the second.

"Pleasure's all mine," he said. "Outta town, huh? What

brings you here all the way from Portland?"

Candi shot her a look. But Maggie knew he'd find out on his own soon enough.

"Just visiting. I'm interested in Wolfe Creek. I'm a writer." *Where the hell did that come from?*

"Writing a book? What kind of book?"

"Not a book. I'm a copywriter. But I *am* interested in the town. Maybe someday I'll write something for your tourism bureau." This was rich. The last thing she needed was for anyone to think she'd be writing an exposé about this place, and whether or not there was a murderer living in its midst. But she needed a solid reason to be poking around other than Aimee, and it'd just popped out.

He spit another stream of juice. "*What* tourism bureau?"

"This town is full of history, Mr. Pruit. The Inn itself is no exception. I know there have been several famous visitors over the years, presidents, actors, and I also know people come here just to stay in those rooms. That's interesting, I think. To most people. And there's a county-wide tourism bureau, as well as a state one."

"Huh," he said, skeptically. Candi just stood there with her mouth open. Maggie hadn't mentioned anything before about doing any research for writing. Of course, that's because there hadn't *been* any research. At least not for writing. Maggie painted a smile on, fake though it was.

"I thought you'd be more interested in our legend over that old hotel."

"Legend?"

Candi unwrapped another piece of gum. "Christ. She just got here, Gary. She's going to think this town is full of nut jobs."

Too late, Maggie thought.

Gary Pruit considered that for moment, spit another stream of dark brown juice, and leaned forward in his chair. "She's gonna find out sooner or later."

Maggie stiffened. "Find out what?"

Candi chewed her gum, managing to look seductive in the process. "Don't pay any attention to him," she said, popping a small bubble. "It's just a bunch of bologna. An urban legend or some such nonsense, made up by bored, ignorant locals."

The temperature in the garage seemed to drop a notch. Dark clouds had rolled in, pregnant with rain, and the light changed fast. Maggie didn't like Wolfe Creek in the daytime. At night, it made her want to crawl inside herself, and not come out until dawn.

"Well." Candi broke the awkward silence. "I think we've wasted enough of your time for one evening, Gary." She turned on her heel. "Come on, Maggie. Let's grab that coffee, hon."

Maggie's gaze lingered on the man in the chair before Candi took her by the elbow and guided her quickly out the door.

"Let me guess. You didn't meet that guy because of car problems?" Maggie was surprised to find herself relaxing back into the overstuffed chair in the corner of the small mom-and-pop coffee shop. The soft voices of the people around them faded into the background and became a comforting hum, while a steady evening rain drizzled outside the windows.

She took a sip of her steaming mocha, watching Candi over the rim of the mug. The other woman leaned back, seemingly oblivious to the looks she received from the men in the room. In the dim light, she really was breathtaking. Comfortable in her own skin, she exuded sensuality.

Smiling, Candi took a sip of coffee, before setting it on the table beside her. "Would you believe I have a past?"

"That just means you're interesting."

"Well, that's a nice way to put it, I guess."

"What kind of past?" Maggie asked, liking how it felt to be drinking coffee in a warm room with rain coming down outside.

"Wolfe Creek is a small town, but it's not *that* small. There used to be a strip club out by the freeway."

"Oh?"

"Yeah." Candi hesitated for a second before continuing. "I used to be an exotic dancer."

"Wow."

"It was right out of high school and was an easy way to pay the bills." She shrugged. "It was hard at first, but you get used to it."

Maggie blew on her coffee, not sure what to say.

"Turns out I was pretty good. Paid the bills and then some."

"How long did you do it?"

"I'd love to say I had a sudden attack of morality, but I danced there until they closed the place down a few years ago. Been waitressing ever since. I have a little nest egg, though. Put away for a rainy day. So at least I have something to show for it." She sighed. "Do you think I'm a horrible person now?"

"Of course not," Maggie said, and meant it. Surprised, since her strict Catholic upbringing didn't exactly condone topless dancing. But she and religion had recently had a parting of ways. She was angry at everyone for Aimee's disappearance. Including God. "I don't think you're horrible. It must have taken a lot of courage to do what you did. I admire that."

Candi reached out and patted Maggie's leg, a gesture that made her stiffen, but the other woman didn't seem to notice. "I appreciate that, hon. It was an experience all right, but I wouldn't change any of it. I've watched a lot of *Oprah* in my twenty-eight years, and she'd say it made me who I am. And that's true."

"It must be hard with creeps like that Gary guy never leaving you alone about it."

"Oh, he's a creep all right. But harmless. Gary Pruit can't get a woody without the help of about three Viagra. That's a well-known fact."

They laughed, and a few more people trickled out the door, leaving them alone except for the barista behind the counter. Outside, the wind picked up and the pines swayed like prickly giants who'd had too much to drink.

Silence settled between them, but it was a comfortable one. They sipped their coffee and listened to the rain patter against the window. After a few minutes, Maggie leaned forward, curious.

"I have to ask…you've lived here your whole life," she said. "What do you think of this town? What do you think of the people who live here?"

Candi smiled, her eyes sharp and knowing. She was

no dummy. "You mean, do I know anyone who could have snatched your friend?"

"Not exactly. Well…yes. I guess."

"That's hard to say. I watch the news. I know how these things unfold. It's always the last person you expect. But yes. I have a gut feeling that whoever took her lives here. I've felt that from the beginning."

"Me, too."

"The problem is, when you live in a town this small, everyone protects everyone else. It's not that they're necessarily trying to cover anything up; it's just that I think there's a deep instinct to watch over their own. Do you understand what I'm saying?"

"Yes." The police had told Maggie that, too. Had warned her that talking to anyone in town would backfire eventually. She wondered if it would happen with Candi.

Leaning back, she decided to try a different tactic. Maybe if she came up with some specific people, the need to gossip would kick in.

"There's this guy. He's staying at the Inn right down the hall from me. Native American, long hair, really good-looking. Do you know him?"

A shadow passed over Candi's face, her perfectly tweezed brows coming together to form a wrinkle between them. "I do."

"Who is he?"

"His name is Zane."

Maggie waited, trying to be patient, knowing her relationship with Candi was new and delicate, like spun sugar. It would collapse if she wasn't gentle with it. "Zane?"

"Zane Wolfe."

It took a second for the name to register. "Any relation to Deputy Wolfe from the cafe?"

"Zane is Koda's brother."

That's why they both looked so familiar. The long hair had thrown her off. The leather jacket and worn out jeans, compared to the crisp, official sheriff's department uniform. So different. Masking the now obvious similarities. *Brothers*.

"How well do you know him?"

Candi looked down, the little wrinkle between her brows remaining. "I've been in love with him since the ninth grade," she said. "That's how well."

Chapter Five

Maggie let her words sink in a minute, watching Candi with renewed interest. The other woman fidgeted with the clasp on her tennis bracelet. Even though her gaze was averted, Maggie could tell there was an expression of longing there. It certainly made sense. The guy was drop-dead gorgeous. But that wasn't all. There was something about him that screamed *bad boy*. Danger. Maybe it was the clothes. Or maybe it was the look on his arrestingly handsome face. Whatever it was, she could see how someone could fall for him in such a way as to never really recover.

"Since the ninth grade?" Maggie asked quietly.

Candi nodded, her lashes forming dramatic black smudges beneath lowered eyes. "My home life wasn't great. I got put into foster care after junior high. Zane and Koda's aunt took me in." She looked up. "Too much information for a coffee date?"

"No, it's okay. You can tell me."

"I haven't talked about it in so long. Whenever I do, it kind of takes me by surprise. All those old feelings come up again."

Maggie waited, feeling a surge of emotion for this woman whom she barely knew. There was pain here. And she identified with pain.

"The state bounced me around for a few months before Ara found me," Candi said. "At that point I didn't even know how to boil an egg. I was always dirty. I remember that. Aunt A, she took me out and bought me new clothes, showed me how to fix my hair and nails, cooked for me."

Ara. Maggie blinked, thinking of the nice lady behind the counter at the Inn. *You'll need a jacket, honey. It's cold out.* This was the woman who had taken Candi in. And for a second, everything was clearer. Everybody in Wolfe Creek seemed connected somehow. They were like pieces of a jigsaw puzzle that, when put together, formed a detailed picture of life in a very small town.

"She must have cared for you very much," Maggie said.

"She's the only mother I've ever known. The only *real* mother. Before I came to Ara, I was a pissed-off train wreck. Who knows if I'd have even made it to fifteen? She loved me so much, I don't think I had any choice but to love her right back. She never agreed with the stripping later on, but it was the best I could do to help out with the bills." Candi smiled. "Anyway, that's when I met Zane and Koda. She was raising them, too. She's had them since they were babies, barely old enough to crawl."

"Are they twins?"

"Koda's older, but only by a year. You'd never know it, though. He's an old soul, always has been."

Koda. The tall deputy with the striking features that made her toes curl. He'd looked serious and drawn when Maggie had met him that day. She'd chalked it up to a cop thing. But there was probably more there. Much more, by the sound of it.

"He's always running around after Zane to keep him from making the next big mistake. Trying to keep him out of trouble. Koda got into a lot of fights at school over his baby brother." Candi's smile widened at this, and Maggie couldn't help but smile, too. "You should have seen them. These two skinny Indian boys, one hell-bent on taking on the world, the other hell-bent on protecting him from it."

"And you liked Zane? Right away?"

Candi looked at Maggie, her eyes twinkling, her earrings glinting merrily. "Who *wouldn't* like Zane right away?"

Maggie kept her mouth shut.

"He's kind of like…" She paused, looking past Maggie now, into the night beyond the foggy windowpane. "He's kind of like this force to be reckoned with. He draws you in before you even know what's happened. Or, at least, that's how it was with me."

"Did you…date?"

"Not sure you could call it that. It was the summer between our junior and senior years in high school. One day he just looked at me *different*. Out of the blue. He didn't even have to work at getting me into bed. We couldn't keep our hands off each other for months. We were joined at the hip." She winked. "So to speak."

"Have you been together since?"

"Oh, no. There've been others in between breakups and jail time. The most persistent is one of Koda's cop friends,

Alan. He asked me out just the other day, but I think he knows there's no real chance. Someday Zane will straighten out and want to settle down. And when he does, I'll be there."

Maggie swallowed. "Jail time?"

"A long time ago, Zane's trouble making caught up and Koda was too late to help." Candi looked pensive. "He started changing after high school. He'd disappear for long stretches of time, never told anyone where he was going or when he'd be back. Drove poor A crazy with worry. Koda worse." She paused, taking another sip of coffee. "I never understood how he could hurt us like that. Especially me."

"Of course."

"Then one day, we got word that he'd stabbed somebody up north in a bar fight. Zane says it was self-defense, and maybe it was. But the guy almost died. Zane did six years. Hard time."

Maggie's mouth went slack.

"When he came back, he was different. *Really* different."

"Different, how?"

Candi frowned and leaned away.

"I'm sorry. I shouldn't push."

"No," Candi said, running her fingers lightly across her cleavage, as if making sure it was still there. "I don't mind. I like talking to you. It feels like I've known you forever."

It was such an open, honest statement, that Maggie felt it tug at her heartstrings. "Me, too." It wasn't a lie. She felt a connection with Candi, though why, she had no idea. She'd never been the kind to believe in fate and chance encounters. She supposed her mother was responsible for that. Things were what they were. Period.

But she was comfortable around this woman with the

makeup and big hair. She was more comfortable with her than she'd been with anyone for a long time. Though she'd be hard-pressed to admit it, it almost felt like moments of talking with Aimee. And again, there was the familiar, unrelenting ache.

Candi smiled, and the glow was back. "Good." Crossing her long legs, she set her mug on the table and wiped the lipstick off the rim. "How long do you think you'll be in Wolfe Creek, Maggie?"

Maggie knew she should be vague and distant just like she'd planned. But something about Candi made her want to confide in someone. A friend. She'd only been in town for a few days, but the remoteness was already wearing on her.

"As long as it takes."

"Really?"

Maggie nodded.

"If you don't mind me asking, how can you do that? Don't you have responsibilities at home? A job, a family?"

"I do. I do have all that. But I have a responsibility to Aimee, too."

"And that stuff about writing something for the tourism bureau?"

"That was mostly for Gary's benefit. Don't think it worked, though. He might be smarter than he looks."

"Doubt it."

Maggie smiled. "It's an interesting town, though. I didn't lie about that. I came here prepared to hate everything about it. But it hasn't exactly worked out that way. It's strange."

"This place grows on you," Candi said. "If you really pay attention, you'll see that most people here had a chance to leave at one point and make a life somewhere else. But they didn't. And the ones who do end up leaving always seem to come back."

Maggie looked up and noticed the barista watching them while wiping down the counter.

"I think someone's listening," Maggie whispered.

Candi looked over Maggie's shoulder and wiggled her fingers. "Don't worry about her," she said under her breath. "But you're gonna run into people who don't like you, for no other reason than you're from out of town."

"You seem awfully friendly."

"Well, I'm an ex-stripper who wears my heart on my sleeve. What can I say?"

Laughing, Maggie set her mug down. She was as full of coffee as she'd ever been. If she kept laughing, even a little, she was going to wet her pants. "Where's the bathroom?"

"Down that hall, first door on the left."

Maggie stood. "Be right back."

The unisex bathroom was warm and cheerful. Small black-and-white photos of Paris and Rome hung on the walls and made it feel surprisingly exotic, as did a vase of dried flowers on the sink. But it was still a public restroom, and Maggie had developed a phobia of them since Aimee's disappearance.

She dried her hands, tossed the paper towel in the garbage, and opened the door with her sleeve pulled over her fist, something her mother had taught her by the tender age of five. A rule of thumb when using the public potty that was right up there with "Don't lick the walls." It had stuck.

"Germaphobe?"

Startled, Maggie looked up to see Koda Wolfe leaning against the wall. The expression on his face was so like his brother's that for a second she just stood there, caught off guard. His starched, long-sleeved uniform shirt fit like a glove and hinted at a nice physique underneath. The silver star on his chest practically glowed in the subdued light of the hallway, reminding her that he was in a position of universal power, no matter how small the town. She tried to think of something witty to say, but all that would come out was, "Uhh…"

His lips tilted. Not quite a smile, but not a frown, either. He looked different than he had at the café yesterday. Standing across from her now, close enough to reach out and touch if she'd wanted to, he almost seemed approachable. Almost.

"I was just using the bathroom," she said. *Brilliant.*

"I see that. But I don't think you want to go out there quite yet."

His face was perfection. Had she noticed just how perfect yesterday? Maybe it was the way he was looking at her, like they were sharing some kind of private joke. Hesitant, she smiled up at him, drawn in by those dark eyes. By the way he seemed to be leaning toward her, just a little.

"I don't?"

It wasn't her imagination. He *was* leaning toward her. And all of a sudden, it was hard to take a full breath.

He reached out as if to put an arm around her waist. She could feel the heat of his breath against her face. *What the…?*

"Not unless you want to drag this along."

He pulled something from the back of her jeans.

Maggie looked down to see a feathery strip of toilet paper in his hand. It took a second for this to sink in.

"Oh…my God."

"Yeah."

If there had been a hole anywhere near, she would have happily crawled in to die.

"Thank you," she mumbled.

He stepped aside, letting her pass without another word. Which was just fine with her. She had no desire to make small talk with a man who'd just plucked Charmin from her jeans.

Maggie made it back to her chair with her cheeks still burning. She must have looked uptight because Candi frowned.

"What?"

"Oh, nothing. But I'd better get going." The urge to leave the coffee shop at nothing less than a sprint was overwhelming.

"Why? Besides, Koda just came in. He'll be back in a second. You can say hi."

"I kind of already did. We bumped into each other in the bathroom."

"Oh. That's great, because you guys didn't get off to the best start yesterday."

Maggie looked at her shoes, not trusting herself with the toilet-paper story without laughing. Or crying. Or both.

"He's not a bad guy," Candi continued, mistaking the look on Maggie's face for something else. "He's really just a teddy bear underneath."

Maggie wondered what else might be underneath before she could help it.

"Koda." Candi glanced over Maggie's shoulder and waved him over. She stood, adjusting the skirt, which had crept up her thighs. "Want to hang out for a minute?"

Maggie watched as Candi gave him a kiss on the cheek. She felt like an outsider. Which, of course she was.

"Can't. I'm on patrol. But I'm glad I ran into you." His gaze shifted toward Maggie.

"Yeah?"

"Aunt A is making dinner tomorrow. Wanted to see if you'd come."

"Of course. Should I bring anything?"

"Just yourself."

"You know," Candi said, stepping back, "Maggie's staying at the Inn. She doesn't really know anyone in town yet. I'd love to bring her, if that's okay."

Horrified, Maggie stared at her. "Um…uh…I wouldn't want to—"

Koda cut her off. "I really don't think that's a good idea." His demeanor went rigid again. Formal. Apparently without toilet paper in the mix, he was going to be a tough nut to crack. "We wouldn't want her to feel like a fifth wheel."

Maggie shot him a look. It was one thing for her to say it. Another for him to. She wasn't nearly as stubborn as her mother, but she'd never been one to back down from a challenge, either. And he was starting to represent a hell of one.

"Nonsense," Candi said. "I know Aunt A wouldn't mind. I'll call her tonight."

Frowning, he put a hand on the back of his neck and rubbed methodically. "I don't think—"

"I'd love to," Maggie said, and smiled sweetly.

Chapter Six

Koda watched Maggie Sullivan walk out the door, not thinking about the way her green eyes had looked just now, or the way her hair corkscrewed about her face. Or the way those jeans cupped her slender backside.

Mostly, he just wanted to throttle her.

"Well, *that* was rude." Candi swatted his arm.

"Rude, how? She's staying right across the street. She doesn't need an escort to walk across the damn street." Unable to help it, he looked out the window at her retreating form. Actually, she probably did need an escort.

"There's a murderer on the loose, or have you forgotten? Besides, isn't it in your job description to protect us female folk?" She batted her lashes, coaxing a reluctant smile from his lips. She was always teasing, always trying to get him to loosen up.

"Maybe I should try protecting you from yourself," he said.

"What's that supposed to mean?"

"It means, you don't need to be involved in this."

"In what?"

"You know what."

"I like her. I like talking to her. Is that so bad?"

"*Yes.*"

"Why?"

"Because she's here to prove that someone in this town murdered Aimee Styles, that's why."

"I think someone in this town *did* murder Aimee Styles, and you do, too," Candi said, whispering for the barista's benefit. "Maybe y'all could use a little help."

He bristled. "Help? From *her*?"

"She's not an idiot, Koda. Would it kill you to help her out? Maybe she'll see a different angle or something. Something you missed."

"Please."

Candi tilted her chin. He knew her well enough to see she was done talking about it. "Well, I like her. And it's been a long time since I've had a girlfriend around here. I get so tired of men trying to decide what's best for me. And that includes you, mister."

"Candi—"

"Don't want to hear it. I'll be there tomorrow night, and so will Maggie. Get used to it."

Grabbing her keys from the table, she threw her purse over her shoulder and walked out the door, leaving him standing there wondering what just happened.

Koda Wolfe didn't mind working nights. Actually, he kind of liked it. He was an introvert by nature and the darkness and chill that fell over the small town as dusk crept in suited his personality just fine.

He sat in his SUV now, his sheepskin-lined jacket pulled high around his neck, and listened to the occasional voices coming through the radio. It was a slow night. He'd stopped patrolling half an hour ago, ending up outside the bar with the motor running, watching and waiting with a resigned look on his face. Sooner or later some drunken idiot would stumble out into the fog and end up peeing on something, fighting someone, or both.

The radio crackled, and he reached over to turn it up.

"Four Victor Ten?" said the dispatcher. Abigail.

"Go ahead," he said, cuing the mic on his shoulder.

"A motorist hit some sort of an animal just south of exit 21. Another motorist called it in. Unknown if you'll need to dispatch."

Koda sighed. He hated shooting half-dead animals on the side of the road. More than likely the driver would be upset. And more than likely it'd be messy.

"Copy. Anyone hurt?"

"Negative. Just shaken up."

"What kind of animal?"

"Said it was a big dog."

"Copy. En route."

"Copy that."

Koda pulled out of the lot and drove slowly through the fog. It had rolled in after the rain and settled so thickly over the streets that in some areas he couldn't see ten feet in front of his vehicle. He passed the bar to his right and hoped that

no one got too stupid tonight. He was the only deputy on
duty this far north, and with this fog, it'd take a while to get
any backup.

By the time he pulled onto the freeway and turned
around in the grassy median, it was shortly after midnight. He
crept along with the light bar flashing an eerie blue and red
into the mist.

Just ahead, he could make out the beginnings of someone's hazards. After putting the SUV into park, he got out
and walked through the freezing night air toward the little
car ahead. The little *yellow* car ahead.

Shit.

Maggie stood beside the passenger door, hugging herself.
She only wore a light sweater, and he could see her shaking
from where he stood. There were obvious tear tracks down
her pale face, and her hair hung in damp clumps against her
neck.

"It was just there," she said, her voice laced with panic.
"It jumped in front of my car."

He stepped close, taking her in, from the top of her
head to her scuffed tennis shoes, completely wrong for winter mountain living. A small cut glistened on her forehead
and was already surrounded by nasty purple swelling. Tears
streaked her cheeks and she wiped them with the back of
her hand. She was a beautiful mess.

He took his jacket off and draped it across her shoulders.

"Hold still," he said, cupping her face. The cut was
deep, but probably wouldn't need stitches, which was good,
because by the time he got her down the mountain, it'd
probably be too late anyway. He looked down into her eyes,
and she stared back. They were wide, but weren't wandering.

She seemed focused. Other than the shivering, she stood straight and still, not swaying at all.

"How do you feel?" he asked.

"It was right here. It was—"

"I'm not concerned about that right now. I'm concerned about you. How do you feel?"

"I…" She sniffed. "My head hurts."

"I know it does. We're gonna take care of that. Do you feel dizzy at all? Nauseous?"

She shook her head.

"Good. That's good." He hadn't realized how tense he'd been until she answered, and he took a deep breath. Even in this day and age, it could be dangerous living this far up. He'd seen people die from car accidents before they could get help fast enough.

Maggie continued staring at him with those scared eyes, and he had a sudden urge to pick her up and carry her to his truck. Away from whatever had run in front of her car and could very easily have killed her. Out of this godforsaken cold-ass night and into somewhere warm and safe. She looked like someone who'd just seen a ghost.

Taking her by the elbow, he led her onto the gravel by the side of the road. It crunched underneath his boots, as if objecting to the weight.

"Now," he said. "Tell me what happened."

"It was right here." She pointed to the front of her car. "I turned around and it was gone."

"What was gone?"

"A big dog. The biggest dog I've ever seen. It was at least waist high." She motioned toward her own hips, which were partially obscured by his jacket. "And it was black. I didn't see it until I was right on it. It came up over the hood and then rolled off to the side of the road. I *saw* it. I got out of the car and came around, and it looked dead. It was bloody. And wasn't moving."

He looked at the hood of the car, which bore no marks, no dents whatsoever, and then narrowed his eyes at her. She might have hit her head harder than he'd thought.

"A car passed and I turned around, and it was…gone. *Gone.*"

He walked over and kneeled in front of the fender. She followed so closely that he could feel her heat, smell her scent.

He ran his hand along the chrome, leaving a clear trail in the grime. No dent. No hair. No blood.

He looked up, and her face contorted. "I hit something. You believe me, don't you?"

"I believe you hit something. But it obviously wasn't hard enough to kill it. Or even injure it that badly if it was able to get up and run away."

"But it *was* injured. I saw it."

"Maybe you clipped a bear or something. It might have been able to withstand a nudge with a car." Even as he said it, he didn't believe it. Hitting a bear, even a small one, would have left some kind of mark on the car.

"It wasn't a nudge, Deputy."

Blood trickled from the cut on her head as if to emphasize her point, and he sighed. "No, I guess it wasn't."

"Then what the hell happened?"

"I don't know. I wasn't driving."

She looked over her shoulder into the woods. "Whatever I hit is hurt somewhere out there. It's got to be."

He knew where this was going. *Christ.*

"We can't just leave it out there to die."

"Sure we can," he said, standing up. "I'm going to drive you back to the Inn. You can come back tomorrow and pick up your car. There's a good shoulder here. It'll be fine."

"Deputy." She grabbed his arm. The feel of her hand through his uniform sleeve was almost hot, in stark contrast to the bitter cold they were standing in. "Please."

He turned, prepared to tell her to get her ass in the truck. Prepared to make her, if necessary. It was cold, and he was tired of standing out here on the side of the road. But the look on her face made him stop.

"Please. I can't leave it out there, hurt. Will you just check? And then I'll go. I promise."

They considered each other for a long moment. Koda could think of a hundred reasons why he shouldn't venture into those woods, and just one why he should. And she was standing there now, freezing, bleeding, and looking stubbornly tenacious. For some reason that touched some deep, primal part of himself. He admired that tenacity. As incredibly maddening as it was.

"All right," he said. "Crap. All right. I'll go take a look. But you're going to sit in the truck where it's safe, got it?"

"Got it."

A smiled bloomed across her face, transforming it into something reserved for magazine pages and movie screens. His chest tightened. If she'd asked him to run to the equator and back, he'd do it, or gladly die trying.

He opened the door and she climbed in, her feet slipping on the icy running board. He reached out to steady her and grabbed her hip. His face warmed. He'd meant to take her elbow.

She shrugged his coat off. "You'll probably want this back."

He took it, aware that she'd only been wearing it for a few minutes and it still smelled incredible. "Stay right here, understand?"

"Yes."

He leaned across and retrieved his rifle from the backseat, brushing her arm in the process. She caught his eye, and it was as if she pulled away from him.

"I'll be right back."

She flinched, and again he wondered how hard she'd hit her head.

"You sure you're okay?"

"I'm fine."

He let his gaze drop to her lips, where she kept wetting them with her tongue. She was scared. That much was obvious. What he couldn't understand was why it was having such a powerful effect on him. Again, he had the urge to take her away from here. From whatever was causing that panicked look in her eyes. But she wanted him to take a look. And for some reason, he couldn't seem to tell her no. So he would. And then he could get her back to the Inn, where she'd at least be warm again.

Nodding, he closed the door and turned toward the tree line, which was only a few yards away. The spaces between the frosty pines were dark and gaping. Sinister. He swallowed. He'd grown up here, born and raised. When you were a Tututni Indian, you were expected to be comfortable with the forest. At one with it, in the daylight as well as night. And mostly, he was.

But honestly, the woods around here were spooky as shit.

He looked over his shoulder and saw Maggie peering out the window, her face a pale moon behind the foggy glass. She wiggled her fingers at him, and he waved back, suddenly feeling ridiculous. He was a Deep Water County sheriff's deputy. He'd seen murderers, rapists, rabid wild animals, car accidents, train wrecks, and one helicopter crash. He could certainly handle going in there to find one injured dog.

Clenching his jaw, he clicked on his flashlight. Holding it in one hand and his rifle in the other, he walked down the slight embankment, careful not to slip and fall on his ass. He could almost feel the weight of Maggie's stare on his back. It wasn't like he was trying to impress this girl. That was stupid. However, he *would* like to keep from shooting himself in the balls in front of her. That'd be nice.

He stepped inside the woods following the strong blue beam of the flashlight. It didn't cut through the fog, so much as illuminate it. The forest floor was damp and spongy underneath Koda's boots, and moisture dripped from the trees around him. Somewhere in the distance, an owl hooted, and chills rose up the back of his neck.

"Here, puppy, puppy…"

The woods smelled wet. The scent of pine mingled with that of moist bark and moss. Koda looked around, sweeping the beam of the flashlight back and forth. The owl hooted again.

"Here, puppy."

Off to his right, a twig snapped.

"Dog?"

Silence. Even the owl didn't answer this time, and the

goose bumps that had risen on Koda's neck, now crept onto his scalp. He took a step forward, his boots sinking into the soggy forest floor. "Where are you, boy?"

Some Tututni. Spooked by a poor animal with a broken leg. But even as he thought it, he knew it wasn't the dog that had him spooked.

"Pup?" Koda's finger hugged the rifle trigger. "Come on."

Snap. Another twig broke, this time closer.

An icy drop of condensation landed on the back of his neck. Koda stared into the darkness where the sound had come from, forcing himself to hold still.

Something was there with him. He was sure of it now.

The legend. It was the one thought that crouched at the edge of his mind, always there, always stalking his subconscious. Some crazy urban legend about Wolfe Creek that had somehow managed to survive all these years. He knew better, of course. But sometimes despite that, it got the best of him.

"Come out, come out, wherever you are," he said, sweeping the flashlight to the left. Then to the right, the barrel of his rifle, a rigid iron finger pointing at the unknown.

And then, from somewhere deep in the belly of the mountain night, was a low rumble. He froze. It was a warning. Instinctually he knew that, just like he knew if he took another step, he might not be fast enough to shoot whatever it was in the cover of those trees and shrubs. A cougar maybe? A bear? It sure as hell wasn't any fucking dog.

Koda swallowed and lowered his head.

"Okay," he said. "Okay. I'm going to back up now."

Cradling the rifle in his arm, he took a cautious step

backward.

Silence.

"That wasn't so bad, was it?"

The owl called again, but farther away this time. He took another step backward, aware of the sweat trickling between his shoulder blades. It was starting to itch, and a hot pressure mounted at his temples.

"There we go." Another step. Then another. After a minute, the sweet sound of a car passing on the freeway signaled he was finally out the way he'd come.

He stood at the tree line, staring into the darkness, and lowered the flashlight to his side.

"Son of a bitch," he muttered.

Chapter Seven

They drove back to the Inn with the fog lifting a little. There were even a few patches above where tiny glittering stars punctured the black-velvet sky.

Maggie's head hurt. Actually, that was an understatement. It throbbed with an intensity that made it hard to form a coherent thought.

She snuck a look in Koda's direction. The darkness inside the sheriff's vehicle made it hard to see his expression. He stared straight ahead, his messy black hair sticking straight up where it hadn't before. Apparently she wasn't the only one whose coif was affected by the relentless damp around here. In spite of herself, she laughed.

He looked over. "What?"

"Nothing."

"What is it?"

"Nothing. It's just…" She pointed at this head. "Your hair."

Craning his neck, he looked in the rearview mirror and smiled. They were passing underneath a streetlamp, and his face was illuminated for a moment. Dimples, smooth olive skin, straight white teeth, expressive crinkles at the corners of his eyes. For a painful second, Maggie's heart stopped. He was *that* handsome. That exotic-looking, with his high cheekbones and wide mouth. And she could see the resemblance again, between him and his brother. It wasn't surprising that Candi had fallen for one of the Wolfe brothers in high school. At seventeen, Maggie would have been a goner, too.

He reached up and ruffled his hair. "It's the mist. It does this."

"I get it."

"Some days I don't even comb it. There's no point."

"I've only been here a few days and I'm starting to think I should invest in a hat. I look like Medusa—" He turned, and she touched her curls self-consciously— "...Snakes. You know."

"No." He held her gaze a little longer than someone driving a car probably should have. "I like your hair."

When it came to Maggie's hair, she knew better. But his voice, which had dropped an octave, was so soft and believable, that she simply stared at him.

A charged silence settled between them, before he cleared his throat and looked at the road again.

"How's your head?" he asked.

"It hurts."

They turned a corner, and there was the Inn. It seemed to be waiting patiently by the side of the road, the porch light burning through the darkness to guide them home.

Koda put the truck in park and came around to help

Maggie out. She was still unsteady, and wobbled a little.

"Whoa," he said, taking her arm. "Got it?"

Her pulse quickened at the touch. "Yeah. Thanks."

"You know, I never asked before. But what were you doing driving around up there in the middle of the night, anyway?"

Maggie shrugged.

"Because," he continued, "this isn't exactly the kind of place where you go exploring on your own."

"I couldn't sleep."

"So you decided to take a drive in the fog and ice? At midnight?"

Shrugging again, she pulled away.

"Hey." He grabbed her arm. "I'm not kidding."

"I know, Deputy. You're *very* serious."

"You think this is some kind of joke? Some kind of game you're playing?"

He was getting mad now. And that annoyed her. He'd just said he liked her hair.

"Yes. I think this is some kind of game. It's so fun that I lost my best friend, quit my job, and moved here to try and find out what happened to her. Fun, fun, fun." She was surprised to find she was on the verge of tears.

He took a visible breath. "You may not want to believe this, but we do know what we're doing. We're not a bunch of hicks in charge of this case, no matter what you might think."

"I don't think—"

"Ah, save it. You've been on TV, remember? You've been quoted in national newspapers saying we aren't doing enough."

"Well, saying you aren't doing enough and saying you

don't know what you're doing are two different things. I *don't* think you're doing enough."

"Oh, really. And what would you do differently in your infinite wisdom?"

Her face warmed. He had her there, and it stung. She wasn't a cop. She was just a person who wanted answers. Desperately.

"For starters," she bit out, "I wouldn't have shut out Aimee's closest friend from the beginning. Has it ever occurred to you that I might have been able to help in some way right after her disappearance?"

"You were a *suspect* right after her disappearance."

"That was routine." Her head swam, and she just wanted to lie down. "The sergeant from OSP said so."

He reached out to steady her again, but she shrugged him off.

He stood there with his hand suspended in the air. When he dropped it, he looked tired. And older.

"As a sheriff's deputy in this county, I feel like it's my responsibility to tell you you're being careless and stupid."

She glared at him.

"Like I said before," he went on, "it's a free country and I *can't* tell you to leave. But I *can* make it my mission in life to follow your every move."

"You're going to stalk me?"

"I'm going to try and make sure you don't get yourself killed."

She bit her tongue. This man had seen her with a toilet-paper tail. Technically, there was a limit to how mad she could get without picturing that debacle.

"What's it going to take to convince you that what you're

doing is dangerous? Whoever took Aimee is still out there. You don't think they might know you're looking? You've only advertised it to the whole fucking country. You don't think they might take exception to that?"

He was right. Of course he was. She could add him to the list of people who thought she was insane, along with her mother. But she couldn't explain, even though she knew it was stupid and careless, she couldn't *not* be here.

She had to find out what happened to Aimee, even if it meant being bait to do it. And maybe that's all it would come down to in the end. Baiting the murderer and flushing him out. But at what expense? Her life?

"Koda?" The front door opened and Ara stepped out in her bathrobe. "Is everything okay?"

Koda gave Maggie a hard look. "Everything's fine, Aunt A. Maggie here had a little accident. I was just driving her home."

"Oh, no." Ara shuffled over in her slippers. "Are you all right?"

"I just hit my head. But it's okay, it's a really hard head."

Ara winced and inspected the cut. "Let's get you cleaned up." She took Maggie's hand and tugged her toward the door. The feel of Ara's warm skin on hers was comforting, and for a blessed second, Maggie forgot all about the mysterious animal she'd hit half an hour before, and the argument she'd just been having with the exasperating man beside her.

She could use a little comfort.

The next morning dawned clear and cold. Outside Maggie's

window, came the rhythmic, *chop, chop, chop* that she'd grown accustomed to over the last few days.

She swung her legs out of bed, grimacing when her feet touched the chilly wood floor. She grabbed her robe, wrapped it around herself, and walked over to the window.

Jim, the caretaker, was in the backyard again, chopping and stacking wood. He stilled and lifted his head, almost as if sniffing the morning air. He turned and looked up, waving when he saw her peeking around the curtains. Lifting a tentative hand, she waved back. How in the world had he known she was there?

He went back to work, raising the ax with his powerful arms, and bringing it down to split the big hunk of wood on the block. *Crack!*

Maggie watched, brushing her fingers across the cut on her head, sore now, and warm to the touch. *Crack!* After another few seconds, she blinked and forced herself to turn away. She grabbed a sweater, a pair of jeans, and her shower bag, and opened the door. Peeking out, she looked both ways before scurrying down the hall to the bathroom. No way did she want to run into Zane Wolfe and his devastating smile this morning.

When she got to the bathroom, she locked the door and leaned against the pedestal sink. The floor tiles were warm, as if someone had been there recently. Maggie reached over and turned the water on in the claw-foot tub, and it came out instantly steaming.

"Ouch!" She snatched her fingers away and blew on them. Wincing, she adjusted the faucet and stood to take her robe off. It slipped from her shoulders and fell to the floor in a fluffy terry cloth puddle. Despite the strong, perfumed bath salts gracing the table by the tub, the bathroom itself smelled like wet pine needles.

Maggie wrinkled her nose and stepped in, taking a minute to get used to the heat. After a second, she sank down, letting the water lap over her thighs and belly. Sighing, she closed her eyes and laid her head back against the cool porcelain.

She'd completely relaxed when a door slammed down the hall. Startled, she opened her eyes. Heavy, purposeful footsteps grew closer. She looked over to make sure the door was locked before turning off the water. *Does Jim have a master key?* She pictured him earlier with the ax poised in his thick hands.

Residual water dripped from the faucet, echoing the beat of her heart.

The footsteps slowed as they neared. Maggie stared at the sliver of light beneath the bathroom door. And then, just like a scene out of a horror movie, a shadow appeared.

Someone stood on the other side of the door.

She tried to take a breath, but found it next to impossible. *So what?* she tried reasoning with herself. *Just because someone's standing outside doesn't mean they're here to murder me. Maybe they just have to pee, Maggie.*

But Koda's words from the night before kept trotting through her head. *You're being careless and stupid…*

Maggie's eyes began to water. It felt like they were actually bugging out of her head. He was right, wasn't he? Whoever had taken Aimee was probably more than aware of Maggie Sullivan's presence in Wolfe Creek. And whoever had taken Aimee had already shown they had no intention of giving her back. Or even offering up a clue of where she might be. Someone like that wouldn't hesitate to do it again. Especially if it meant shutting Maggie up.

Gripping the sides of the tub, she cleared her throat. "Can I have some privacy please? I'll be out in a minute."

That is, if I live through this bath. Maybe she'd have to reconsider. Maybe she'd have to pack up and get her rear end home before someone collected it for a trophy.

But even sitting there, starting to shiver, as much from fear as the dropping water temperature, she knew she couldn't do that. Because obsession drove her now. The all-consuming need to know what had happened to her friend. She honestly didn't think she could live with not knowing. Had that ever really been an option?

As she watched the shadow at the bottom of the door, teeth rattling away, she thought of her mother and the last thing she'd said before her only daughter had left for the little town high in the mountains of Oregon. *Promise me you'll be careful.*

And then, as if on cue, the shadow shifted, the floorboards creaked, and whoever it was took a step away. Then another, and another, until the shadow passed gracefully by, and Maggie Sullivan, the careless stupid girl from the city, was left alone again in her cold, lonely bath.

Chapter Eight

Maggie walked down the staircase that evening, her fingers trailing along the old wood banister, glossy with varnish yet rough at the same time. There was probably a story behind each knick and scratch, and the history geek in her was endlessly fascinated by this.

Candi waited on the first floor, wearing a long coat with a faux-rabbit-fur collar. Her cheeks were flushed neon pink.

"It's colder than a witch's tit in a brass bra out there."

Maggie snickered, surprised to find how glad she was to see her new friend.

"I heard you had some trouble last night," Candi said, putting an easy arm around Maggie. "And it looks like it kicked your ass, too."

Maggie moved her hair carefully over the cut.

"It's not that bad, sweetie," Candi said. "I've had boy-friends give me worse."

They walked into the dining room, where Ara met them

wearing a red-checked apron that said *Kiss The Cook!*

"Well, there they are!" She gave Candi a quick hug, before fussing over Maggie. "I was worried about you. Feeling any better?"

Maggie was ashamed for having been so rude to Ara before, who practically oozed hospitality like a warm peach cobbler.

"Much, thanks for asking. And thank you for taking such good care of me last night."

"I'm just glad you weren't hurt any worse. Please," she said, motioning toward the table, "sit."

"Where are the guys?" Candi asked.

"I haven't heard from Zane yet. I'm assuming he'll be here. That boy hasn't missed a meal in his life. Koda's on his way. He's running late with some sort of sheriff's business."

She disappeared into the kitchen and as if on cue, Koda walked in. It was the first time Maggie had seen him in civilian clothes. He looked over and she remembered to smile, thank God. Worn, sexy Levis hung loose on his hips. His blue-plaid shirt was open at the throat, showcasing smooth, dark skin and a corded, muscular neck. His hands were buried in his pockets and his broad shoulders were hunched a little, masking his considerable height. Maggie stared up at him.

Candi elbowed her in the ribs.

"Uh...hi. Hi," she said.

Koda leaned over to kiss Candi's cheek, eyeing Maggie over the bouffant strawberry-blond hair. "Hi, hi to you, too."

Maggie's face burned. She'd always been painfully aware of her slender body, her plain looks. But never in her life had she been more self-conscious than around boys in high school. She had to remind herself that she wasn't that girl anymore. She was a grown woman who'd filled out since those awkward teenage years. (Not a lot, but she'd take what she could get.) She was smart and sassy. Full of moxie, that was what her brothers said. Aimee had always said she was full of shit.

Remembering her friend, and how she probably would have taken great delight in Maggie's nervousness around Koda Wolfe, Maggie pushed her shoulders back.

None of this was lost on Candi, however, who looked amused.

From inside the kitchen, Ara banged around, pots and pans jostling together in a cacophony of dinnertime sounds. She sang a low tune, the words of which Maggie couldn't hear. The warm, savory smell of meat cooking filled her senses and her stomach growled in response.

"How're you feeling, Maggie?" Koda asked, his eyes settling on the cut at her hairline.

"Just fine, thank you."

"I was hoping you'd come to your senses today."

"If that means giving up on looking for Aimee, sorry. No way."

"Well, obviously I use the word 'senses' loosely."

She gave him a dirty look.

"Guys," Candi said. "Chill out."

Maggie sat stiff in her chair. "Tell him. He's the one try-ing to bully me into leaving."

"And she's the one who's going to get herself killed," Koda snapped back.

"Like you care," Maggie said.

"I do care. You getting killed means more paperwork for me."

"*Koda*," Candi cried.

"You're unbelievable," Maggie said.

"You're crazy."

"Stop it, you two."

Feeling bad for Candi but unable to help it, Maggie fired back. "Tell me you wouldn't do exactly the same thing if it was someone you loved."

He stared at her, his expression icy.

"Well, well, well." They all looked up to see Zane standing there. "Glad I got here when I did. Is this a lover's quarrel?"

"Shut up, Zane," Koda grumbled.

Maggie's cheeks caught fire.

Beside her, Candi seemed all too aware of the other male who had so quietly entered the room. Not that Maggie could blame her. Zane Wolfe was full of grace and sexuality.

His long black hair hung forward. His bomber jacket, which he wore over a faded Led Zeppelin T-shirt, creaked like saddle leather when he moved. He was clean-shaven tonight, with only the shadowy promise of a beard along his jawline. And when he smiled at the two women in the room, his teeth flashed bone white against his skin.

From across the table, Maggie could feel the hostility in Koda's very presence. But there was something else there, too. Something that made her stomach flutter.

Zane pulled up a chair and sat down as if he had nothing better to do.

"Where've you been?" Candi's voice was suddenly bedroom silk, cascading into the room like a long dark ribbon.

"Here and there."

Maggie shifted at the electricity in the room. Something

was obviously still going on between the ex-stripper and the Native American hottie who sat across from her. She glanced across the room to find Koda staring at her. His gaze drew her in, and time seemed to slow. It wasn't animosity in his eyes, now, but something that made her want to stare back. To give in to this new and powerful intimacy between them.

It was mind-boggling, her sudden shift of emotion toward all of the people there. They were so complex, so dynamic, and so different than what she thought she'd encounter when she arrived in Wolfe Creek, that for a second, she was overwhelmed by it.

She looked up to find Zane staring, too. His black eyes were bright, glittering. His mouth was turned up on one side, his head cocked as if he knew her exact thoughts. He was such a curious mixture of intensity and nonchalance, that she had trouble sitting still under his obvious scrutiny.

Candi must have noticed, because she cleared her throat with a little too much enthusiasm. "I don't know about you all, but I'm starving."

Zane's gaze slid to her and dropped to her cleavage. "Me, too."

Maggie blushed, embarrassed. Candi didn't seem to mind, though. She leaned forward and Zane grinned in appreciation. Koda muttered something under his breath.

Balancing a platter in both hands, Ara burst through the door. "I hope everyone's ready for some roast beast!" Koda got up to help, and she patted his cheek gratefully. "Zane," she said, "glad you could make it, honey."

He rose to give her a hug. "I wouldn't miss it."

"I thought we'd see more of you when you moved in, not less." She clucked affectionately and reached up to move his hair from his face. Then gasped. *"Zane."*

The table grew silent. Now that his hair was brushed back, Maggie could see a bruise covered the entire side of his face, a deep, angry color that bloomed even under his olive complexion.

"What happened?" Ara asked softly.

"Nothing. Just a little disagreement. You should see the other guy."

Koda rubbed his temple. "Should we even ask if you're hurt anywhere else?"

"Nowhere a little TLC won't fix," he said, winking at Candi.

She wasn't smiling back. "Zane?"

"I'm fine."

"Are you sure?" This, from Ara, who no longer looked cheerful. In fact, she looked like all the life had been drained right out of her.

"Aunt A, I'm *fine*. It was nothing."

"You promised. You promised you'd stay out of trouble."

"I didn't go looking for it. It found me."

Ara's face reddened. "You're violating your parole. Or haven't you thought of that? You're putting your brother in a terrible position. Or haven't you thought of that, either?"

Zane sighed.

"We're worried about you," Candi said. "One of these days you're gonna pick a fight with someone faster."

"Or someone with a bigger knife," Koda said.

"Will everyone *please*, just get off my back?"

"And what about the other guy?" Koda asked. "How's he?"

Zane gave his brother a hard look. "He's fine, bro. And

by fine, I mean he's not dead."

"Well, that's a relief. Because the next time you go back, it may not be for any piddly fucking six-year sentence."

Maggie had the feeling that she was witnessing much more family dynamic than met the eye, and her throat tightened. Even with the scent of warm roast beef hanging in the air, she was no longer hungry.

"Look at me," Ara said.

The chilly look Zane had just given his brother was gone. In its place was one of complete indifference.

"I want you to stay away from that bar." Ara's voice was no longer sweet and passive. It rang with a tone that made Maggie want to shrink away. "We all know it turns you into something you're not."

Zane gazed down at her defiantly.

"I love you too much to lose you again. Those are my conditions. Either live by them, or you'll have to find somewhere else to stay."

Tension hung in the room, heavy and thick. Finally, Zane leaned down and placed a gentle kiss on Ara's cheek.

"I just remembered," he said, rubbing his chest. "I have somewhere to be. I'll see y'all soon."

He turned and disappeared out the door, a soft zephyr that had breezed through, touched them briefly, and vanished before they'd even known what happened.

Chapter Nine

It was clear and cold outside the Inn. The three-quarter moon hung suspended in the star-studded sky, lighting up the darkness in a crazy silver glow. A beautiful night.

Hunching her shoulders, Maggie walked in silence next to Koda down the bumpy, cracked sidewalk of Main Street.

After Zane had walked out of the dining room earlier, the atmosphere had deteriorated in a matter of seconds. Candi had begun to cry, and Koda had risen to put his arms around his aunt's shoulders, who stood staring after Zane as if unable to believe he'd gone.

"He'll be back," Koda had said. "He always comes back."

"But what if he doesn't?" Ara's voice had stirred something inside Maggie's heart. "How many times will we have to wonder?"

"He's too much of a pain in the ass to *not* come back."

But Maggie had noticed a deep frown had settled over his mouth.

"Let's hope so," Ara had said. "For his sake."

The rest of the evening had passed uneventfully. Candi said her good-byes shortly after dinner, refusing Koda's offer of a stroll around the block. *It's clear,* he'd said. *No fog, no rain. No telling when we might see the sky again.*

Maggie supposed it might have been his way of trying to make things better again. She was beginning to see this was part of his very nature. The peacemaker. The one who made things right for everyone.

Ara had also turned him down, and after hugging them all good night, had headed somberly upstairs.

Koda kicked a rock now, and it went tumbling down the sidewalk and into the gutter. Maggie glanced at him, but he didn't look back. He seemed lost in thought, his face smooth and expressionless.

"You know," she said, breaking the silence, "Aimee was a wild child, too."

He turned toward her, his eyes shining in the moonlight. "Yeah?"

"She was always staying out all night, going with guys she didn't know. Making her parents crazy. Trying to drag me along with her."

She now had his full attention, but she kept her head down, watching one of her sneaker laces bounce along the cement.

"I know," he said. "I've read the OSP reports. But honestly, I'm surprised to hear you say it. You've never mentioned it on TV or in the papers when you described her. Or your friendship with her. And some of that stuff was pretty in-depth."

Maggie glanced over, her mouth going dry. She hadn't

meant to bring Aimee up, and now that she had, felt the need to defend her. "I couldn't bear the thought of them saying she might have run off or that she went willingly with someone and might have deserved what happened. Even so, they dug up some things and tried to hint at it. She didn't go willingly, Deputy. And she sure didn't deserve what happened to her."

"I know she didn't."

Those four little words covered her like a warm blanket. It felt good to have him on her side, even if it was just this one small admission.

They walked in silence for a minute longer, their breath crystallizing in the air.

"You know," he finally said. "We've had dinner together. You've witnessed my little brother's total lack of common sense, and you've eaten my aunt's world-famous roast beef. I think you can probably stop calling me Deputy, now."

She smiled. "Does this mean we're friends?"

"Let's not push it."

"Acquaintances?"

"Consider yourself lucky. I don't make acquaintances easily."

"Neither do I."

"*No*."

"What's that supposed to mean?" she said, shivering despite her down jacket. "I'm so nice. You just have to get to know me. Funny, too. The whole package, really."

"I'll take your word for it."

Is he flirting with me? She slid him a look, resisting the urge to elbow him in the ribs.

"But you also have a rather large chip on your shoulder,"

he added.

"Wouldn't you? Under the circumstances?"

"Yes. But I wouldn't necessarily ride into town hell-bent on proving that everyone here is a murderer."

"I'm not."

"Oh, come on. Tell me you're not just itching to accuse the first hillbilly you see who didn't have an alibi that night."

"Not true."

"Is true."

"No." Frustrated, she crossed her arms over her chest and took a deep breath. "Can we please just call a truce and agree to disagree on some of this stuff that doesn't really matter? Maybe we can work as a team to try and find out what happened to Aimee."

Stopping, she turned to him. For a second he just stood there, staring up at the moon. Then he faced her. "I've been thinking a lot since last night," he said. "You were right. We shouldn't have cut you out of the investigation altogether. I think, under the right circumstances, you might be able to help a little. *If* I decide to work closer with you on this, you'll have to listen when I tell you to back off. Got it?"

Maggie beamed. For the first time since arriving in Wolfe Creek, she felt a faint glimmer of hope. Like she might not end up flopping around like a fish out of water after all. Candi had said the deputies around here might be able to help. And she'd been right.

She nodded, wanting to hug him.

"And this is more of an OSP and FBI investigation at this point than anything else. You have to accept that. We're *assisting*. Those guys don't like their toes stepped on. It doesn't do to piss them off. Understand?"

"Yes. Perfectly."

"One more thing. And you're probably not gonna like this one."

"Anything." Maggie trembled.

"If you're going to be my sounding board on some of these theories, you're going to have to try and see this from a cop's point of view. Not a friend's. You've got to try and see the big picture."

"Yes. I—"

He cut her off. "You *have* to open your mind to the possibility of things not happening that night like you thought."

Maggie understood. He wanted her to be prepared for a rough ride and a painful ending. As incredibly difficult as that might be.

"I'll be open-minded. I promise."

His face relaxed a little. "Good."

"Thank you, Koda. Can I still call you Koda?"

"We've had dinner together. It seems weird for you to call me Deputy now."

Grinning, she rubbed her hands together. "Where do we start?"

"We start by not telling anyone we had this conversation. Even though I think most people in this town are good people, your hillbilly assessment was fairly on the money. There are some folks who wouldn't like it if they knew you were being given information about this case."

Goose bumps that had nothing to do with the cold sprouted along Maggie's arms. And there it was again. A warning. She found herself wondering just what they would do if they found out. It scared her. Plenty. But she did feel a little safer as an acquaintance of Koda Wolfe's. And without thinking about it, she stepped closer. The constant feeling of being watched was always stronger next to these woods.

"The less digging you do on your own, the better," he said. "We need to be smart about this. I'm not going to jeopardize your safety, period."

"Got it."

"Okay."

She was trying to keep her teeth from chattering.

"Cold?"

"A little." *What a lie.* She was freezing her privates off out here.

"Should probably think about heading down the mountain to get some warmer clothes if you're going to be spending the winter here," he said, looking at her shoes.

"What? You don't like Sketchers?"

"I don't like the thought of your toes falling off from frost bite, no."

"Why thank you, Deputy Wolfe. As much as I like to shop, and I *do* like to shop, that would require me to get in my car again, and I'm traumatized for life."

Frowning, he eyed the cut on her forehead. "I guess you would be. If you're worried about it, you could always go with Candi. She heads that way every now and then."

Maggie nodded. The thought of hanging out with Candi for a few hours sounded good. She hadn't really prepared herself for how lonely this adventure was going to be. Even now she was dreading going back to her room at the Inn with only the nightmares to keep her company.

She wiggled her toes. They'd passed numb ten minutes ago and were now working on frozen. Next up? Boots and cozy socks. Things were slowly looking up. Maybe, just maybe, she'd end up accomplishing something by coming here after all.

"Can I ask you something?" she said, as they turned to walk back the way they'd come.

"Shoot." He was closer than before, his arm brushing her shoulder. The feel of it warmed her everywhere, and before she could help it, she was wondering how his bare skin would feel next to hers.

"What's this legend I've been hearing about?" She looked over, so engrossed in his profile that she tripped over a bump in the sidewalk.

Koda took her elbow, his hand strong and reassuring. "You okay?"

She nodded, embarrassed.

"The legend. God. Who told you about that?"

"I went with Candi to the mechanic's. He said something about it."

"I'm surprised she didn't tell you."

"She said it was an urban legend and not to pay any attention to it."

"Huh. I doubt she'd admit it, but I think she believes some of it herself. This is a small, isolated town, Maggie. People here can be...superstitious."

It was the first time he'd called her by name. She snuck a glance in his direction again. He was so striking under the light of the moon that she had to consciously look away or risk falling flat on her face.

"What about you?" she asked. "Are you superstitious?"

He paused, and for a second, the only sound was that of their shoes scuffing the cement. "It depends on what you mean," he finally said. "I wonder about things, yeah. I think that's probably a given, especially coming from a family like ours. You're born with questions, and I guess you never really stop asking."

She glanced over again, confused.

"But I'd try and consider the source, if I were you," he continued. "I wouldn't put too much stock in what you hear from Gary Pruit. The guy practically swims in his Corona."

Maggie laughed. "I got that about him."

Koda smiled, but didn't offer anything more. He obviously wasn't going to elaborate. Maggie considered this for a minute, and couldn't help but see the similarities in Candi's explanation yesterday. Short and sweet, and that was it. Even when they'd had coffee afterward and had plenty of time to talk about it, she didn't mention it again. *Why?*

She balled her hands into fists, caught between not wanting to irritate him, and dying to know. She settled on irritation. A proven Sullivan method.

"So…what exactly is it? Native American folklore?"

He sighed. "Sort of."

"Okay." She waited, but he remained quiet. "And?"

"And, it's just some talk from a bunch of people who sit around drunk in front of campfires."

"Uh-huh. What else?"

Stopping, he turned. "You're not going to let this go."

"Nope."

"You're stubborn. Has anyone ever told you that?"

"I'm Irish. You should meet my mother."

"Ah." He nodded, smiling down at her in the darkness. "So?"

"Fine. *Fine.* The legend…it all goes back to my family. I have ancestors who settled here more than a hundred years ago."

"The photos at the Inn," she said, immediately picturing the couple whose eyes were so haunting. "Are some of those people related to you?"

"They are. My great-great grandfather Bastien settled here before the turn of the century. He was French Canadian. A businessman."

Maggie nodded, captivated.

"He was well off and came to southern Oregon with the intention of developing. You can guess how well that went over. A rich white man wanting to take over Tututni land. I think you could probably have thrown a rock at a hoedown and hit someone who hated him."

"I'm not sure I've ever met anyone who used the word 'hoedown' in a sentence."

"Well, you obviously haven't spent enough time with me, little lady."

She laughed. "Go on."

"Things got worse when he met my great-great grandmother. She was the daughter of the chief. Very beautiful, very willful."

"I've seen the pictures. She was gorgeous. And he was…"

"Powerful," Koda finished. "The story goes that when he saw her for the first time, he fell in love immediately and was obsessed with having her."

Maggie listened, hanging on every word. She'd even forgotten about her frozen toes for a minute before remembering and wiggling them again.

"He convinced her to marry him. Of course this was against the chief's wishes. He was infuriated. The tribe was divided. Some welcomed the marriage, thinking that with her connections to his money, it would trickle down and eventually help their people. Others despised him for taking one of their own, and despised her even more for going willingly."

"Oh my God."

He smiled, and she could clearly see the ancestral resemblance. The same straight nose, high cheekbones, dark eyes as in the photograph. It seemed like his great-great grandmother had spanned the decades to come to rest inside this Indian prince standing right here in front of her. The thought was enough to make her unsteady. Or maybe that was just the bump on her head.

"Right after the marriage, she started showing with her first baby. The chief supposedly said that if his daughter was going to dilute the Tututni blood by allowing a white man to father her children, then the children would pay. The family would suffer."

Maggie shivered.

"And that's where it gets weird." He raised his brows. "Still want to hear?"

"Yes. Go on, please."

"The story goes that with the help of an old woman who practiced witchcraft outside the tribe, he put a curse on their descendants. The sons in particular."

Prickly goose bumps marched up Maggie's legs. "Why the sons?"

"The chief knew that Bastien wanted boys. He wanted sons to carry on his name."

"First the sons, then the town."

Koda nodded. "We can't really understand the level of resentment toward Bastien Wolfe back then. He took over this area. Married a Tututni woman. Had half-breed children."

"Did they have sons right away?"

"Right out of the chute. The baby got sick and died when he was a toddler. They never knew exactly why, but the doctor guessed it had something to do with his heart."

"Oh no."

"His second son died of lupus when he was seventeen."

He must have recognized the troubled look on her face, because he paused, frowning. "Are you sure you want to hear the rest of this? It's just stupid folklore."

"It's not stupid. Go on."

He took a visible breath before continuing. "I don't know if you know anything about lupus, but it's a terrible disease. Attacks your organs. Very painful."

"My aunt had lupus," Maggie said. Her mother's sister, Shannon, who'd lived in Belfast during Maggie's childhood, had recently passed away. Maggie had only met her once when she was eight, and all she remembered was that Shannon had been a small woman with a drawn face. But she clearly remembered her mother telling her how awful the disease was. "It's horrible."

"Yes, it is."

Maggie waited, but he didn't go on. "What?"

"Do you know what lupus means in Latin?"

She felt her toes curl.

"It means wolf," he said.

And just like that, she wanted to squirm out of her skin. As if on cue, a coyote yipped from somewhere up the mountain.

"Holy shit," she whispered. "Are you saying the chief's

curse turned out to be an honest-to-God disease?"

He tipped his face toward the pale, frigid moon that hung suspended above. "It's a little worse than that."

"What could be worse than your family being cursed with lupus?"

He looked down at her, his eyes narrowing, his lips curving slightly, and a small breeze rustled through the bushes behind them.

"Being cursed as a werewolf," he said.

Chapter Ten

Maggie stared at him, taking a moment to process what he'd just said. "What?"

"You heard me."

She forced a laugh. The temperature seemed to have dropped in the last ten seconds, and she quivered from the chill. "That's the Wolfe Creek legend? Werewolves?"

"Yup."

It was something out of a child's fairy tale. *I'll huff and I'll puff, and I'll…*

Shrugging, he turned and crossed the street toward the Inn. "I told you it was ridiculous."

"Wait." She said, rushing after him. "Wait a minute. You can't just leave it at that. You skipped over a whole century. What happened after the second son died from lupus?"

"Ahh, I see I've drawn you in, young lassie," he said in an accent almost as good as her mother's. "Tomorrow you'll get to hear all about Big Foot and the Loch Ness *Monster*."

She grinned. "I want you to finish. Please?"

Surprising her, he took her hand and brushed his thumb over the backs of her fingers. "You're cold."

His hand warmed hers, and heat crept up her arm. A curl of desire took her by surprise.

"Okay, I'll finish," he said, his voice low and suggestive. "But I might get you home after curfew. Aunt A might notice."

"I'll take my chances."

He let go of her hand, and she immediately missed the connection, the intimacy of his gesture.

"Where was I?"

"The second son."

"Ah. Well, he wasn't the only one who's died from lupus."

"Oh, no. How many?"

"A fair amount. And it's not very common for men. It mostly affects women. But the cases in my family have all been men, and they seem to have gotten worse over the years."

"How does that tie in to *werewolves*?"

"Who knows? Maybe the chief and his buddy thought they'd come up with a disease that would allow us Wolfe's to experience the ultimate in pain and suffering. That's how the legend goes, anyway. That we get sick and go through some kind of transformation."

She nibbled a fingernail. "Why is it called lupus? Why wolf?"

"Sometimes people with lupus get a rash on their face. It's like a mask. It looks like a wolf, or so they say." He shifted from foot to foot. "Back in the day, the pain medication was practically nil and it wasn't uncommon to hear people cry out and moan from inside their houses. Or even howl."

"Good Lord."

"So what do you think, lassie?" Koda asked, the new nickname gentle and teasing, and stroking something inside her. But there was an underlying tone in his voice, too. "Still gonna stick around?"

"Of course," she answered a little too quickly. As if trying to convince herself, as much as him. "You're not saying people actually believe that stuff, are you?"

"Oh, they believe it, all right. They might not admit it right away, but get a few beers down someone and you'll hear all kinds of interesting things."

"Are you speaking from experience?"

"Yes, ma'am. I haven't always been with the department. I was young once, too. There's not a whole lot to do in a town this size when you're twenty-two, except drink. I've spent my fair share of time in a bar."

They considered each other for a long, quiet moment. Koda Wolfe's eyes were as dark as the shadows that stretched out behind him, and just as deep.

"This is you," he said.

Without Maggie realizing it, they'd ended up back at the Inn. Yellow lights glowed in the old, frosted windows.

Turning, she smiled. "Thank you for the walk, Deputy Wolfe."

"Koda," he said.

"Koda."

They stood looking at each other for a long moment, before he leaned so close that she could make out his eyelashes in the dim light.

"I'll see you tomorrow. Sleep tight," he added in a dramatic whisper.

She could still feel the heat of his breath on her cheek as he climbed into his SUV and started the motor. When he pulled away from the curb she waved, watching the taillights gradually fade until they were just a tiny memory of warmth in the clear, cold night.

Trembling, she dipped her chin into her collar. She wasn't sure how she'd sleep tonight.

But wasn't anxious to find out.

"I have to pee." Aimee laughed, but it sounded hollow and far away. It was foggy outside the car, but warm inside, and Maggie had a sudden urge not to stop. If felt safe in there.

Aimee pointed to a sign. The words were big and distorted, and the fog was so thick that Maggie had to slow down to see where she was going.

"There," Aimee said. "Pull over." She laughed again, and the sound broke something deep inside of Maggie. She turned to her friend, but couldn't talk. She could hardly breathe.

The car veered to the right as if it wasn't being driven at all. It seemed to be moving on its own. And Maggie was suddenly angry. So angry that she gripped the steering wheel and shook her head back and forth. But Aimee didn't notice. She kept talking and laughing, asking if Maggie was hungry, maybe they should stop and eat something.

The woods here were the darkest Maggie had ever seen. The trees towered over them, and it seemed like they were alive, watching the car pass beneath.

Even though she didn't see any other cars, no other people through the fog, she knew they weren't alone. The smell of smoke and pine filled her nose, making her gag.

"He bites," Aimee said.

She turned to her friend, who was staring at her. She wasn't laughing anymore. She looked scared. Her eyes were wide and her mouth hung open. There was drool coming out the side.

"What?" Maggie asked. Aimee didn't look like herself. Her eyes were vacant. She wasn't making any sense.

"He bites," Aimee said again. She was now staring past her, out the window. Maggie turned to look. Nothing but fog. Beyond that, darkness.

"You're scaring me," Maggie said. "Stop it."

Then her eyes settled on Maggie. They weren't blue anymore. They were black.

"He's going to get you," she said.

"Who?" Maggie asked, and started to cry. She felt like she might wet herself. "Who's going to get me?"

Aimee smiled. Her teeth were crooked and yellow. She was an old woman now, her hair hanging in stringy white tendrils past her bony shoulders. She lifted a gnarled hand and pointed a finger at Maggie's heart.

"The boogeyman," she whispered.

Maggie woke with a gasp and sat up in bed. The room was dark and cold, the clock on the dresser reading 3:05 a.m.

Her hair stuck to her neck in a floppy, sweaty mess.

The boogeyman.

She shook her head, desperate to clear it. Aimee had been trying to warn her.

He bites.

Maggie swung her legs out of bed. She needed a drink of water.

Not bothering with her robe, she opened the creaky door and peered down the hallway. *Empty*. Of course it was empty. It was three o' clock in the morning. But the dream was still fresh and she felt the need to look just the same.

She walked down the hall toward the bathroom, her bare feet padding along on the worn, flower print carpet. An elderly couple had checked in yesterday and were staying a few rooms down. Maggie glanced at their door as she passed. As far as she knew, they were the only ones staying at the Inn besides her and Zane. Ara, of course slept downstairs in the quarters off the kitchen. Jim, the caretaker had an apartment above the carriage house out back. Still, the place seemed deserted. Strangely silent.

Stepping onto the chilly bathroom tiles, Maggie closed the door. She turned on the faucet and leaned down to scoop some water into her mouth, then splashed a little on her face. She grabbed a paper towel and straightened to look at her reflection in the mirror.

The dark circles underneath her eyes made her look five years older. So did the way her mouth was drawn into a grave frown. Her typically pale skin was even more so, making the scattered freckles across her nose stand out like brown confetti.

She wadded up the paper towel, tossed it in the garbage, and leaned against the sink. Her heart had finally slowed to a normal rhythm after the nightmare, but she still felt jumpy. She closed her eyes and forced a deep breath, then another. If she didn't get a grip fairly soon, she'd have to take one of the crazy pills the doctor prescribed after Aimee had disappeared.

She'd spent too many weeks in a haze because of those pills and didn't really want to rely on them now just when she needed to be at her sharpest. Still, the thought of taking one and being able to sleep soundly until morning sounded pretty good.

Opening her eyes, she concentrated on the ancient lilac print wallpaper over the tub. She wondered how long it had been there. As long as the tub itself? It was possible. This place had seen more than its share of guests. More than its share of seasons. Gloomy autumns, which would transform themselves year after year into winters that were thick with snow and silence. And then spring would come again, and she imagined it would be beautiful here.

She'd only been back in Wolfe Creek for a little over a week, but was already starting to feel some kind of connection to this place. To the people, whom she was surprised to find that she not only liked, but liked to spend time with. History, that was messy and sad, but also laced with passion and love. Those things were starting to pull her in. To affect her in ways she hadn't expected. She felt confused and overwhelmed. Exhausted.

Opening the bathroom door, she squinted into the hallway. The events of the last few days kept playing over and over in her head. Coffee with Candi, hitting the dog, the stalker at the bathroom door, dinner at the Inn, the walk with Koda. They all swirled around and around and around, until she was having trouble keeping them all straight.

She hurried back to her room and locked the door with both hands. Plucking her makeup bag from the dresser, she rooted inside until she came up with a small plastic baggie. Inside were a few tiny pills, an insurance policy she was now grateful she'd thought of.

She placed one on her tongue and swallowed it dry, feeling its sharp little edges scratch the back of her throat as it went down.

Licking her lips, she walked to the window, drawing the curtains to look up at the moon, which cast an eerie luminescence over the yard below. The ax that Jim used every morning was stuck in the stump as if suspended midblow. The rickety gate hung open, sagging away from the fence on rusty hinges. And beyond that, the forest. The ever-present forest, with its secrets and fine gray mist.

Maggie felt a chill at the same moment she noticed her brain begin to go slightly fuzzy. Maybe it was wishful thinking, but her stomach was empty and the pill would probably work fast. She blinked, her eyelids heavy. Good, she was getting sleepy. She needed at least one night's sleep without waking in a sweaty panic. Tomorrow she'd do without. But tonight she needed rest.

She began to turn away but froze when something caught her eye. She wiped a quick circle into the foggy glass and looked down at the yard.

It was empty. Completely still. With her pulse fluttering in her neck, she squeezed the curtain in her fist.

After a long minute, she began to turn again. And again, there it was. *There.* Right by the gate.

Something big and dark crouched on the other side of the fence. She could see it now and her scalp prickled.

What in God's name is that?

An animal of some sort. She was sure of that much. Two

bright eyes looked out from a giant, black mass of a head. But the shape of it, the curve of its body was harder to make out.

Maggie stood there, dazed. The pill was definitely taking effect. She put a hand on the sill to steady herself. Whatever it was saw the movement in the window and looked up. The silence in the room was deafening.

She took an involuntary step back. It seemed to be looking right through her. A memory from her childhood came rushing back then. Maggie licked her lips, seeing it unfold, vivid and clear as if it'd happened just yesterday. Her parents had taken her to the zoo when she'd been a toddler. They'd been standing in front of the big-cat enclosure and her mother had taken her hand, leading her up to the smudged glass. *Cougars*. She could still see the eyes, the whiskers, the twitching ears, soft and deceptive. She remembered wanting to touch them. *Isn't he pretty?* Her mother had said. *Look at his tail*. Maggie had turned to see another one, a bigger one, crouching just a few feet beyond the glass. Her jewel eyes had been fixed on Maggie in such a way that even in her babyhood, she'd been instinctually afraid. The cougar had wiggled her bottom, just like a housecat that was stalking something small and weak. The muscles and bones of her powerful haunches rippled beneath an iridescent hide. And then she'd pounced. Hitting the glass with such force that it shook. Maggie could still hear the *thud,* her mother's sharp intake of breath, feel her arms scooping her up and holding her close. And Maggie had cried then. Big, hiccupping sobs. She'd been inconsolable and had hated the zoo ever since.

She blinked now, unable to look away from whatever it was in the yard, and was suddenly very glad she was on the second floor. She couldn't shake the image of the cougar. Or that unmistakable feeling it had wanted to eat her for lunch.

Maggie took a breath. Watching, waiting. And then, just like that, the dark shape whipped around, fast as a lightning bolt in a stormy sky. There was a rustle of leaves, and it was gone.

Trembling, she gripped the windowsill and stared at the empty yard below.

She felt strange all of a sudden. Almost detached, like she was standing outside her own body. Watching herself at the window, a thin ghost of a girl in a T-shirt and sweats, with dark circles underneath haunted green eyes.

And wondered if she'd really seen anything at all.

Chapter Eleven

Koda drove slowly down one of the back roads of town, his SUV rocking over the deep grooves in the packed gravel.

Abigail was talking through the radio, something about an accident up the freeway. But for once, Koda wasn't paying attention. And it wasn't just because this particular call was out of his jurisdiction, either. He was thinking about something else. Someone he couldn't quite shake, and was finding he didn't really want to.

It was official. Maggie Sullivan had worked her way under his skin. Now he just had to figure out what he was going to do about it.

Not even a week ago, he'd been annoyed at her nerve, showing up here and nosing around like she owned the place.

But last night, not only had he agreed to keep her involved in the investigation, he'd also had the urge to plant a kiss on those impossibly pink lips. *What the hell?* Men thought with their junk and Koda was no exception. But he'd always prided himself on being smarter than his little brother and most of the guys in town, who would sleep with just about anyone who passed by. Just because a girl was attractive didn't mean he was going to go screwing her brains out. At least not before the one-*week* mark.

But Maggie… Maggie was different. Tough and obstinate, yet vulnerable in a way that made him want to walk closer on an evening stroll, just so she might feel safe. Or make her laugh only to see that mouth relax into an easy smile. She was maybe one of the most pensive people he'd ever met, but there was a definite spark behind her eyes. A spark that had probably always been there, but had no doubt grown dimmer over the last year.

"Four Victor Ten."

Abigail again. She sounded urgent, slightly off-key, which was rare for her. And this time she was talking to him.

"Go ahead."

"We have a cold home invasion and assault at sixty four South Glen, apartment B."

Candi. Koda swallowed the suddenly sour taste in his mouth and had to force himself to reply. "Injuries?"

There was a moment's hesitation at the other end of the radio. Again, rare. "Affirm. Female caller reports that she's bleeding heavily from the head. Medical en route."

The ambulance would be coming from Splendor Pass, the town directly South of Wolfe Creek, which had the nearest hospital. Koda glanced at the clock on the dash. 8:14 a.m. It usually took at least twenty minutes and that was with decent weather. With the drizzle and light fog rolling in, it could be longer.

"Copy. En route. Suspect on scene?"

"Negative, as far as she knows. Sending backup."

That might take just as long as medical.

He gunned the engine, kicking up dense chunks of mud and gravel behind the SUV. Whatever bleeding there was, it would be up to him to stop it, or at least slow it down until the ambulance got there.

God, let her be okay.

Koda looked at the clock again.

Hang on, Candi.

Blood everywhere.

Koda stepped inside with his GLOCK drawn, avoiding a shattered lamp on the floor. He scanned the dim room. The curtains were still closed and the only light was coming from the bedroom down the hall.

"Candi?"

Bloody fingerprints on the walls, streaks on the throw rug. Puddles and specks on the hardwood floor that he tried to step around.

The neighbor's dog barked relentlessly in the next apartment, setting his hair on end.

"Candi?"

Someone moaned from down the hall.

Koda turned the corner, his gut coiled, his breathing shallow.

And there she was. Lying in a heap next to the wall, the phone still in her hand. Her hair was matted in bloody clumps next to her face, which was a swollen, purple mass. Her normally wide eyes were no more than slits beneath her brows.

"*Shit.*"

Her head flopped to the side.

"I'm here, baby," he said, dropping to one knee. "I'm here."

She moaned again. There was a nasty gash on her forehead, already starting to clot. Most of the blood had probably come from her nose, which looked broken.

"Whoever did this," he said, "are they still here?"

"Don't...think so."

Koda tensed and beads of sweat trickled down his temples. Never in his life had he wanted to kill someone more than at that very moment. Every muscle in his body strained against his skin. His clothes were tight and hot, his shoulders stretching the fabric of his uniform shirt until he thought it might rip.

Carefully holstering the gun, he took off his jacket and covered her with it. She was starting to shake. Not wanting to move her, but knowing he should at least elevate her legs, he got up to get a pillow from the bed.

After he grabbed two, something small fell from the folds of the fabric and landed at his feet. Koda leaned down to pick it up. A lighter. With embossing. Without thinking, he stuck it in his pocket and turned back to Candi.

He lifted her feet as gently as he could and slid the pillows underneath.

"The ambulance is on its way. They'll be here any minute."

One eye tried to open, tried to look up at him, and he had to clench his teeth to avoid biting his tongue. He picked up her hand and cradled it to his chest.

"You should see the other guy," she said.

He forced a smile. "That's Zane's line."

And then the wail of a siren. Faint at first, but growing louder, stronger by the second.

Maggie sat in the parlor with a fire popping merrily off to the side. She'd just gotten off the phone with her mother who had asked for the one-millionth time when she was going to give up already and come home.

"Not until my money runs out, Mom. I told you."

There'd been an exasperated sigh on the other end of the line. Maggie knew better than to go over the reasons again. She'd done that before, and to no avail. She didn't expect anyone to understand, least of all her hardheaded, overly rational mother. This *was* craziness. She knew that. But she also knew that for the first time since arriving in Wolfe Creek, she might be a little closer to some answers. And that was good enough for now.

She'd finally hung up after telling Mary Sullivan that she loved her and promising again to be careful.

Maggie sat now, sipping a cup of tea and listening to the elderly woman across from her.

"This Inn is just lovely, isn't it?" the woman said, shaking her head of cottony curls.

"It is," Maggie agreed.

"So much to absorb." She grinned, the lines in her face exploding into dozens, upon dozens of crinkles. "I'm a retired history teacher. I can't get enough of this kind of thing."

Maggie smiled.

"Your room is just down the hall from ours, isn't it?" The

woman, whose name was Vera, leaned forward and gazed at Maggie. She couldn't have been a day younger than eighty, but her sharp gray eyes missed nothing.

"It is. I think we share a bathroom."

"Yes, we do. I heard someone walking down the hall early this morning. I suppose that was you."

"I hope I didn't wake you up."

Vera shook her head, her delicate earrings winking in the firelight. "Oh, no. I was having trouble sleeping." She leaned closer and Maggie could now see a curious silver ring around her irises. It gave them the appearance of glowing in the dimly lit room. "I was hearing things," she said quietly. "Things outside the hotel."

"What kinds of things?"

"Twigs breaking, scratching..."

Maggie shifted, uneasy.

"I hear things most people can't." Vera sat back, her orange lips tilting slightly. "I can almost feel them, if that makes sense."

"Ahh," Maggie said, and for the first time wondered if the kindly woman across from her wasn't playing with a full deck.

"Oh, I know it sounds strange. Most people think I'm crazy. That's okay."

"I don't...I didn't..."

"It's all right. Most of the time I keep my mouth shut. My husband hates it when I tell people like this, and mostly I don't. Not anymore. But you..." Her eyes narrowed. "I think you might feel things, too."

Maggie didn't know what to say. *Feel things?* What things? She looked at Vera, drawn in by her strange eyes.

"Let me ask you this," the other woman said. "Did you see anything last night?"

"I'm sorry?"

"When you were looking out the window?"

A tingle crept up Maggie's neck. How in the world could she know about that?

"I told you," Vera said. "I feel things."

Apparently she can read minds, too. Maggie laughed nervously.

"Did you? See anything?" Vera asked again.

"I did." The room seemed chillier, even with the crackling fire. "I saw some sort of animal by the fence. But it was too dark to make out what it was. Did you see it, too?"

"I didn't have to see it. I knew it was there. That's what was keeping me awake."

Vera's response was oddly casual. *Weird.* This was the kind of conversation someone should be having in a whacked-out dream after a spicy meal. Not in broad daylight with a retired history teacher.

"Ready, darling?"

Maggie looked up to see an older gentleman crossing the room toward them.

"Bud, come meet Maggie Sullivan. We've been having a nice chat."

Bud took her hand and gave a formal bow. "Miss Sullivan, charmed."

She liked these two. Boring, they were not. "It's nice to meet you."

"I hope my wife hasn't been keeping you hostage. She does like to talk about these old places."

Vera shot Maggie a look. Clearly, she wanted to keep

this particular conversation between the girls.

"Oh, no. I've been enjoying it."

He helped his wife to her feet. "We really should get going, my love."

"Yes, we should." Vera smiled down at Maggie. "We're on our way to California to visit our son and his family. We have a new grandbaby as of last month."

"Congratulations. I hope you have a nice trip. It was wonderful meeting you both."

"Likewise, dear."

With Bud safely out of earshot, Vera bent close. "You be careful, you hear? Especially at night."

Before Maggie could respond, she had already gone, leaving a perfume scented trail in her wake.

Chapter Twelve

The sounds were coming from the dining room. A shout of some sort, and then a crash against the wall.

Maggie had been sitting in the parlor watching the fire fade to embers when she heard it.

She jumped and scooted to the edge of her chair.

"I'll kill him!" a male voice boomed. "I'll fucking *kill* him!"

Maggie rose and walked hesitantly toward the dining area.

"No! No, don't tell me to calm down." This voice was the loudest, punctuated every now and then by two others.

Slowly, she peeked around the corner to see Zane, Koda, and Ara standing there. Ara covering her mouth, Koda with one hand flattened against Zane's chest. The men looked volatile. But something about Zane's posture, something about the look on his face, made Maggie question being in his vicinity.

Before she could turn back around, he spotted her.

"Well, well, look who's here," he said.

"Stop it, Zane," Ara said.

"Where do you think you're going?" he continued, his voice dripping with animosity. "You should be hearing this, too. Since it's probably your fault in the first place."

"*Zane*," Koda growled.

Leaning into Koda's stiffened arm, Zane glared at her. His eyes were bloodshot and glassy, like he hadn't slept all night. "No. She should know. Or are we making sure she's sheltered from all of this, Koda?"

"Shut up."

Maggie swallowed hard before finding the courage to speak. "What happened?"

"Candi was attacked this morning. She's in the hospital." Ara walked over and put an arm around Maggie's shoulders. "Don't pay attention to him. This isn't your fault."

"Like hell it isn't," Zane snapped. "Everyone knows how this fucking town operates. Someone saw Candi talking to Nancy Drew over here and decided to shut her up."

"That's an awfully big assumption," Koda said.

Zane turned on him. "Why don't you just admit you're protecting her? You said yourself she has no business here. You said it just a few days ago. What happened between then and now to make you change your mind?"

His black gaze settled on Maggie. "Never mind," he said. "I can guess what happened."

Her face burned as if someone were holding a torch to it.

"Zane," Koda said, "if you don't shut your mouth right now, I'm going to shut it for you."

"Don't bother." Zane shoved his brother's hand away and stalked past. "I'll kill whoever it was," he said over his shoulder. "Watch me."

And then he was gone.

Ara leaned against the table. "Sweet Jesus."

"It's okay," Koda said. "We'll get whoever did this. He's not going to kill anyone."

Shaking her head, Ara stared at him. "What's happening around here, Koda?"

"I don't know. But we're going to find out."

The room spun, dizziness making Maggie's stomach lurch, and she braced a hand on the wall. *I don't know. But we're going to find out.* They were the same words spoken by Alan McCay, the state trooper, the night Aimee disappeared.

I don't know...

And they were just as scary today as they'd been a year ago. Maybe even more so. Was it her fault all these horrible events had been set in motion? Maybe Zane had a point. Maybe she was bad luck to the people of Wolfe Creek. Maybe wherever she went, pain and misery followed. After all, the road trip had been her idea. She had convinced Aimee to come along...

"I'm sorry," she said, her eyes stinging. "I'm so sorry."

Koda looked up. He didn't touch her, but she could tell he wanted to. The thought of being wrapped in his arms was all consuming. He was a virtual stranger. But she wanted his comfort. Needed it.

His face was compassionate, his words soft. "This isn't your fault. Do you understand?"

She nodded, doubtful.

"I need to see her," Ara said, fidgeting with the tablecloth.

"But I can't go until tonight. We have guests coming, and I can't leave until they're checked in."

"That's okay. I'm going this afternoon," Koda said. "She wasn't conscious earlier, but I have to go back and ask her some questions. I'll make sure she's all right. Then I can drive you tonight if you want."

"Jim can take me. But can you tell her I'll be there soon?" The older woman looked close to losing it, which broke Maggie's heart. She thought of the rugged caretaker, and the fact that he was the one Ara wanted to go with. Maybe there was something more here for Jim than just caretaking. Maggie liked the thought of that. Maybe this sweet innkeeper wasn't alone in this big old place after all.

The room grew quiet and the memory of Zane's words still hung in the air.

Maggie studied Koda's profile. His wide, expressive mouth set in a firm line. She wanted to trace his narrow nose, the high forehead, and the strong jaw, peppered with new stubble.

And right then, at that very second, she was forced to recognize a longing inside herself that she wasn't necessarily comfortable with. Not yet. Maybe not ever. But she felt it just the same.

He must have sensed her watching, because he met her gaze.

"Do you want to come, Maggie?"

Dazed, she nodded. "Yes, please."

The long, twisting drive down the mountain had never been Koda's favorite thing in the world. The truth was, he'd seen too many accidents on this road to feel anywhere near complacent. It was a freeway, which also meant it was a thoroughfare for semis and heavy logging trucks that crowded the slow lane, laboring down the mountain with almost as much difficulty as they had climbing it. Their brakes smelled hot and their engines ground away in the lowest gear, sounding like huge, grumpy bears just waking from hibernation.

Koda passed one now that was having a particularly hard time. Smoke billowed out the exhaust pipe, which pointed like a blackened finger to the sky. Its bright yellow hazards flashed ominously, on, off, on, off. All part of living up here. Unless you had a chopper, there was only one way down.

Switching lanes, he glanced over at Maggie, who was looking out her window. She hadn't said more than two words since she'd climbed in. Her curly brown hair hung loose next to her face, hiding it from view.

He focused on the road again, wondering what she was thinking. Guessing he had a pretty good idea.

"He had no right to say that to you."

"Huh?" Maggie turned, her eyes appearing larger than normal. They were round as polished, green stones.

"Zane. He shouldn't have said that."

She considered this for a second, before looking back out the window. "I don't know. Maybe I deserved it," she said. "Maybe what happened was because of me. It makes sense."

"The only person responsible for hurting Candi was the one who broke into her apartment. Zane says a lot of things when he's mad. He talks out his ass. It's a well known fact, ask anyone."

This coaxed a faint smile. "He still has a right to be angry."

"He does. We all do. No one lays a finger on that girl

without paying dearly and that's the God's honest truth. If I find him first, Zane's going to have to settle for the leftovers. But he has no right to be angry with you."

"The last thing I want is to cause problems for anyone here. That was never my intention, I hope you know that."

She fidgeted, wringing her hands together in her lap. Her fingers were long and elegant. Sexy. He imagined them wrapping around him, stroking his—

He shifted in the seat and focused on the road again.

"When I decided to come here," she continued, "I guess I was only thinking of myself. How things would affect me. I never considered anyone else."

"That's what happens when someone's grieving a loss. They're kind of selfish that way."

"I guess. But I can see things more clearly now."

He said nothing. Seeing things clearly might not be such a bad thing. He suspected that she'd been making blind, gut decisions for a while now.

"Honestly," she said, "do you think it's possible that someone attacked Candi because she was talking to me?"

Koda sighed. "It's possible. Anything's possible. But I don't think it's probable."

"Who else would want to hurt her? I can't imagine her having any enemies."

"That's where you're wrong. I'm assuming she told you what she used to do?"

Maggie nodded.

"Well, she hung with a pretty rough crowd. Lots of those guys were obsessed with her. Wouldn't take no for an answer. I could see one or two of them pulling a stunt like this. Especially drunk.

"Wolfe Creek is a great town in a lot of ways, Maggie. There's a reason I haven't moved somewhere else. Somewhere bigger. The family history is one thing. But it's more than that. Once you live here, put down roots, it has a hold on you. You don't *want* to leave."

"I can imagine," she said, facing him now.

"But as great as it is, it can be a hard place, too. There's a lot of poverty, a lot of ignorance. So if you're asking if anyone else had it in for Candi, the answer's yes. I think a number of people could have, and for no good reason, either." He looked over then. "This doesn't have to make sense. Sometimes people do stupid shit. Just because."

She watched him, quiet. Then began fidgeting again.

Without thinking about it, he reached over to still her hand. But instead of letting it go right away, he held on. Her skin was smooth and pliant, warm to the touch. He looked up to see the expression on her face. There was something there that mirrored what he'd felt when he first saw her, although he'd be hard pressed to admit it. He'd felt it again last night when she'd stepped closer on the sidewalk, her arm brushing against his. And he was feeling it now. Her mouth was slightly open, her lips parted in such a way that made him want to lean over and coax them with his tongue. She tightened her fingers around the back of his hand, surprisingly strong and sure of herself, and his face grew hot in response.

A minivan passed on their right, barreling down the mountain and blasting its horn as it went. Koda pressed his foot to the gas and yanked his hand away.

The SUV lurched forward again, as if remembering it had somewhere to be.

Chapter Thirteen

Splendor Pass Community Hospital was tiny compared to most. It really was more of a clinic than anything else. But it was nice, and as Maggie walked through the sliding glass doors a step behind Koda, she was met with a warm blast of air and a pleasant, clean scent.

He'd been quiet since he'd held her hand in the truck. She hadn't said anything either, but her hand still tingled where he'd touched it. In fact, her entire body felt strange, as if she'd just now accepted after a year of denial, that she could still feel this way. It had been so long since she'd focused on anything but grief, that the concept of being attracted to someone was hard to wrap her mind around.

They walked up to the nurse's station, where a young woman sat on the other side of a gleaming counter.

"May I help you?"

Maggie thought she caught a glimpse of appreciation in the other woman's eyes as she settled the brunt of her attention on Koda. He was in uniform, the silver star on his jacket gleaming in the fluorescent light of the lobby.

"We're here to see Candi Brooks," he said.

"Sure thing." Her fingers danced along the keyboard. "Miss Brooks is in room 116."

"Thanks."

The woman watched him turn, her gaze dropping shamelessly to his rear end. Maggie felt a prickle of irritation. *Rude*. Stepping possessively closer to Koda, she glanced at the clerk over her shoulder. Then ran right into him when he stopped to drink from the fountain a few feet away.

"Sorry," she mumbled.

As they climbed the stairs to the second floor, her thoughts turned dark again. For the last hour, she'd been trying to brace herself for seeing poor Candi, but was having a lousy time of it. What if she blamed Maggie, at least in part for what happened? No matter what Koda said, no matter what *anyone* said, no amount of reassuring was going to make her feel okay with this. Because she felt it was her own fault.

Koda read the room numbers aloud as they passed. "One fourteen, one fifteen...here we go."

He hesitated before knocking. She figured she wasn't the only one dreading this.

"Come on in," said a voice from inside.

He pushed the door open, just as a nurse in pink scrubs was leaving.

"She needs her rest," she said, eyeing Koda as if resenting his presence. "I know you have your questions, but please keep it short."

"It's okay. He's family."

Candi lay in a bed by the window, her hand outstretched toward them.

The nurse nodded and walked out the door, closing it behind her.

An awful lump rose in Maggie's throat. Candi's face was a swollen, black-and-blue mess. Her nose was bandaged and part of her hair was shaved away from another bandage on her head. Her beautiful, strawberry-blond hair that had been teased to perfection just last night.

A strangled sound escaped Maggie's throat. Koda stood beside her, his deep complexion drained of color. He moved first, crossing the room to take Candi's hand.

"Don't say it," she said, trying to smile. Her lips were so puffy, they shone like glass. "I look gorgeous, right?"

Koda took an audible breath. Maggie could tell he was trying to compose himself.

"You always look gorgeous."

"Liar."

He smiled down at her, but there was something in his expression Maggie hadn't seen before. An emotion so intense that it twisted her stomach. She had no doubt that whoever did this would pay.

"I'd never lie to you," he said.

"At least I'm finally getting that nose job I've always wanted." The swollen eyes shifted to Maggie. "Hey there, doll."

That was it. Those three little words, warm and sweet, despite everything, were enough to make Maggie want to cry. Her chin trembled, even though she willed it not to. She stepped closer, brushing Koda's shoulder.

"Hi, Candi."

"Why so sad?"

"I'm..." Maggie struggled to find the right thing to say, but it eluded her like a naughty puppy. "I'm so sorry. I'm so sorry this happened to you."

Candi's lips curved. It looked painful. "Me, too. But he didn't hurt anything that won't heal. And on the bright side, I'll have a few days off from the café, right?" She looked back at Koda, who was frowning. "Oh, come on, you two. I'm not *dead.*"

She wasn't dead. Not this time... Koda must have been thinking the same thing, because he slid Maggie a look.

"It's okay," Candi said. "I'm gonna be fine."

Maggie stared at her. "I feel like this could be my fault. Zane—"

Candi put a hand on Maggie's arm. "Don't say anything else. Zane's already been here and I know what he thinks."

"He has a point."

Koda sighed.

"Well, he does," Maggie said.

"Zane's mad," Candi said. "He needs someone to blame, so he's blaming you. When he calms down and thinks it through, he'll realize how stupid that is. But unfortunately, Zane isn't the type to calm down easily."

Maggie remembered how he'd glowered at her that afternoon. Like he'd wanted to come across the table and rip her throat out.

"He'll be fine," Candi went on. "Don't worry about him. You weren't the one who did this."

Maggie could see why men were obsessed with this woman. She was stunning, on the inside and out. And even though Maggie had only known her a short while, she understood this. Accepted it as fact.

"I've been trying to tell her that," Koda said. "But she won't listen to me."

"I listen to you," Maggie said quickly. "I do."

They looked at each other for a long, pregnant moment.

"I'm glad to see you two are getting along," Candi said.

Maggie's face pulsed. Was it that obvious?

"Candi, honey." Koda pulled up a chair. "Do you remember anything? Anything at all?"

"Sure. I remember most of it. Right up until I hit my head, and then it gets foggy. I was just getting out of the shower and I heard someone banging on the front door."

"What time was it?"

"Early. I had to open at the café. About seven."

Koda fished a small notebook out of his jacket pocket and flipped it open. "You opened the door?"

"I went to the door, but I didn't open it. I looked through the peephole and that's when he busted it open. Hit me right in the damn nose."

Koda glanced up, his face drawn. "What did he look like?"

"He was wearing a mask."

"What kind?"

"A Halloween mask. It was one of those things you put over your entire head. Rubber. It was a Native American face. There was long black hair. Feathers in it."

Koda scribbled on the pad, his head bent in concentration. "We found some of the hair on the floor. Synthetic."

"I grabbed it," Candi said. "I tried to get it off, but he kept ducking. He was fast. *Really* fast."

"Did he say anything?"

"Nothing. Not a sound. Not even when I hit him over the head with the lamp."

Koda's lips twitched at that. "How hard?"

"Hard enough to knock him backward. Bastard."

"How about his body type? How big was he?"

"Tall, lean. But he was solid. Strong. He felt like cement."

Koda nodded, scribbling in the notebook. "What was he wearing?"

"Just a T-shirt and jeans. Don't ask me to describe them, because I can't. That's about all I noticed. Except that the T-shirt was white."

Pausing, he looked up. "No jacket?"

"Nope."

"Strange. It was in the teens this morning."

"The whole thing was strange."

"Do you know how long he might have been there? Roughly."

"I passed out after I hit my head. But as far as him beating the shit out of me, I think that part only took a few minutes."

Koda finished writing something down and the room grew quiet, the only sound being the purposeful footsteps of medical staff down the hall.

"Anything else?" he finally asked. "Anything that sticks out about him?"

"Yeah." Candi sniffed, and for the first time, Maggie could tell she was getting tired. They should leave soon. "He smelled funny," she said.

"Funny, how?"

"Don't know if I can put my finger on it. Kind of earthy. But familiar. I can't explain it."

"Earthy...like he needed a shower?"

"No. Earthy, like *earthy*. He smelled sort of like...pine

needles and mud."

Koda glanced at Maggie.

"Okay, then." He patted Candi's leg. "You should rest now. I'll be back later to do a formal interview. Mostly we just wanted to see you. Make sure you're all right. Aunt A is coming later, okay?"

Candi nodded, her eyes heavy. Maggie was surprised she'd managed to stay awake this long. She was probably getting some pretty serious pain meds through her IV. But if Maggie had learned anything about Candi so far, it was that she was one tough cookie.

Maggie leaned down. "Bye, Candi. I'll come back to see you tomorrow."

She smiled, but her eyes were closed.

"Let's go," Koda said quietly. "She's exhausted. We shouldn't have stayed this long."

Maggie followed him to the door just as the nurse came back in, lips pursed.

"We were just leaving," he said.

"Wait." Candi's voice was sleepy but urgent. "I remember something. It's fuzzy. It was after he pushed me…"

Koda stepped forward.

"He took…" Candi's face screwed up. Maggie couldn't tell if it was from pain, or the effort of remembering. "He took my bra," she said. "The son of a bitch took my bra."

The fog had been so thick.

Their little yellow car had inched along, making its way through the mostly deserted town. It was almost midnight and a full moon hung over head. There were moments of clarity, where the mist parted and the moonlight shone through like a giant lamp in the sky.

"I'm about to pop," Aimee had said, and they'd laughed again.

She pushed her hair away from her face, and looked out the window. "This place gives me the creeps, Mags." She said this while rubbing the fog away from the glass. "If I didn't have to go so bad…"

They passed an old mechanic's shop on the right. A post office on the left. There were no other cars, and Maggie felt oddly cold despite the heater blowing warm air against her cheeks.

She leaned forward and rubbed the windshield with her shirtsleeve. "I can barely see."

"Up there," Aimee had said. "To the right. There's a gas station and convenience store."

"Wolfe Creek General Store," the sign had said. As they got closer, they could make out two dejected gas pumps in the gravel parking lot. Beyond that, a small building with a neon-red OPEN sign flickering in the window.

Maggie had pulled up next to a pump and looked at Aimee before opening the door. "At least they're not closed," she'd said. "Otherwise we'd be going on the side of the freeway."

They'd stepped out into the frigid night air, and it had taken Maggie's breath away. Aimee came around and grabbed her elbow. "You sure you don't want to? It's not too late."

"And get hit by a car with my pants down? I'd rather take my chances here."

They'd stood there, arm in arm, staring at the store as if it were a slumbering animal. They couldn't see much beyond the windows, except that the lights were on. An animal cried in the woods behind them and the sound sent chills up Maggie's neck.

Aimee danced from foot to foot. "It's freezing out here. Let's go in."

They opened the cloudy glass door, a bell tinkling their arrival, and were met with a peculiar emptiness. There wasn't a clerk in sight.

"Weird," Aimee whispered. "This place is so weird."

"I know."

Across several aisles of junk food and travel essentials, was the bathroom. There was a crude stick figure of a man and a woman painted on the door.

"I guess that's it," Aimee said.

They heard a clunking sound outside and turned to see an attendant by the pumps.

Maggie sagged in relief. At least it wasn't completely deserted like some kind of Twilight Zone *episode.*

She'd turned to Aimee. "Why don't you go first, and I'll get the gas."

"Okay. Get me a pack of those mini doughnuts, will you? The ones with powdered sugar. I'll pay you back."

"We'll make ourselves sick."

"That's the whole point of a road trip, Mags. Junk food and gossip." She turned then, her hair bouncing down her back in a wave of blond curls, her head tilted just so.

And then she'd looked casually over one shoulder. She'd been so young, so pretty, so full of life.

"I'll be right back," she'd said.

Chapter Fourteen

Maggie sat staring out a window of the Arrowhead Café, the memory of that night thick behind her eyes and her coffee long since cold.

It was October thirtieth. A day that had dawned like any other. Freezing, wet, foggy. But Maggie had risen out of bed with a distinctive weight sitting squarely on her chest. She'd woken crying, which wasn't unusual. But she'd also woken confused. She'd been dreaming about Aimee. She'd been alive and staying with her at the Inn. They'd been drinking a glass of wine in the parlor, talking about Koda Wolfe.

I like him, Aimee had said. *I think he's good for you. I think he can protect you.*

Maggie had leaned forward, but Aimee had begun to swim before her. Maggie narrowed her eyes, struggling to see her friend clearly. *What does that mean? Protect me, how?*

I like him, Aimee had said again. *He'll protect you.*

Maggie had been annoyed. What was she talking about? And then, like the fog itself, Aimee had broken up and disappeared, leaving only emptiness behind.

Aimee? Don't go. Aimee?

"Aimee?" She'd sat up in bed and looked around. She was alone, of course. But the dream had felt so real that it took a moment for her brain to adjust. And then the familiar ache inside her chest, so painful that she thought she might break from it.

She sat in a small corner of the café, thinking of that night like she had so often before. Thinking of the last moment she'd seen her friend alive.

Rubbing her thumb up and down the chilled mug, she stared out the window in a daze.

One year. One full year. And they were no closer to finding out what happened to Aimee today than they'd been that awful, cold night. How could a person just vanish like that?

The door to the café opened, bringing with it a chilly gust of air. Maggie put her hand over her napkin to keep it from fluttering to the floor, but didn't look up.

Aimee.

"Is this seat taken?"

Koda stood over her. He wore a gray North Face fleece and leather boots laced only halfway up. Very outdoorsy. Very sexy. Although he probably just rolled out of bed, he also looked like something out of an Eddie Bauer ad. Her heart squeezed at the sight, confusing her. Making her wish she'd met him in a different time and place. Under different circumstances.

She smiled, all too aware of her wild, unwashed curls

and bare, freckled face. "Please, sit."

He did, scooting in close. She caught his scent, which was clean and warm. Maybe a little aftershave from the day before. "You look tired," he said.

"That's just a nice way of telling someone they look like crap."

"No. You're beautiful. But you do look tired."

She flushed. Compliments from the opposite sex didn't come her way very often. She'd never been the pretty one or the vivacious one. That had been Aimee. Maggie had always been comfortable being the bookworm, the one with the dry sense of humor. The one her mother called, "the personality." But never the pretty one.

If Aimee had been sitting there at that very moment, she would have elbowed Maggie in the ribs and said, *See? I told you.*

"Thank you."

Koda motioned for the waitress. "Coffee please, Eileen. Black."

He glanced around then, nodding to a few men on the other side of the café.

"They're not missing a thing," he said. "We're the talk of the town."

"God. I never wanted that."

"I know you didn't. But the truth is, what's happened is bigger than just you and me."

She knew that. But at the same time wondered if her presence here, along with her new attraction to Koda Wolfe, was like blowing on smoking kindling.

The waitress brought his coffee and studied Maggie with renewed interest, before sauntering away again.

"She's a gossip," Koda said, taking a sip. "But harmless."

"Noted."

They were quiet for a minute and Maggie looked back out the window. There were only a few inches between them. She could have put her hand on his thigh if she'd wanted to.

"I know what day it is," he finally said. His voice was low, hesitant. The mist had turned to a light rain, temporarily washing clean the pickup trucks in the parking lot. The same trucks Maggie had so bitterly sized up a week ago, but now realized were just sensible mountain transportation.

The weight on her chest was crushing. It was hard to breathe. Trying to keep composed, she folded her hands neatly on the table. Still, she couldn't look at him.

"I know how tough this is for you," he said. "I know you don't know me very well. But you can talk to me. I'm a pretty good listener."

She winced and struggled to clear her mind of everything. Of Aimee, and the last image she had of her.

I'll be right back.

"Thank you," she said, her voice breaking. She stared down at her coffee. A year ago it had been wine and girls' nights. Now, it was just stark reality. All of a sudden, she felt too old for her body. "I think I'm going to go back to my room and lie down for a while. I don't feel very good."

He dug a few dollars from his wallet and put them on the table. "I'll walk you," he said.

They opened the door of the café and stepped outside with Maggie squinting into the rain. She walked next to Koda, comforted by his presence. Then, surprising herself, and probably surprising him, too, she slipped her arm in his. He looked down, but she stared straight ahead, not trusting herself to meet his gaze. Instead she moved close, letting his body heat jump the boundaries of her winter clothing. And then after a few steps, he covered her chilly hand with his. It was such an uncomplicated gesture, made with no pretense whatsoever, but one that seemed to express everything left unspoken between them. She was safe while she was with him.

When they got back to the Inn, they were greeted by a roaring fire and the scent of bacon coming from the kitchen. Ara served breakfast to her guests on the weekends, and despite Maggie's gloom, her stomach rumbled.

"Warm up before you go to your room." Koda said gently. "It might do you some good."

She followed him into the parlor, their footsteps creaking on the old wood floor. Maggie held her hands in front of the fire, and Koda leaned against the mantel, his short hair dripping onto his jacket, and watched her.

"Aimee was so fun," she finally said, staring into the licking, popping flames. "You would have liked her."

"I'm sure I would have."

The heat warmed Maggie's face, warmed her chest through the unzipped jacket. Memories, one after another, came rushing back. Riding bikes with Aimee to school, Aimee declaring every Sunday pajama day. Aimee's voice over the phone, Aimee's smile, Aimee's laughter. They were all so vivid, so real, that Maggie had to blink them away.

"It's the not *knowing*. If she suffered, or if she could still be alive somewhere." She turned and looked up at Koda with months of unshed tears finally beginning to spill down her cheeks. "Some days I don't think I can stand it, I miss her so much."

"I know," he said, stepping close. "I know you do."

Before she realized what was happening, he'd pulled her against his chest. She closed her eyes and breathed him in, feeling his heart thud against her cheek.

She wrapped her arms around his waist. He was warm and solid, not an ounce of fat on his lean frame.

He touched her hair, ran his hand down her back, and she shivered in response.

And then he was pulling away, his hands on her shoulders, his breath tickling her face. She looked up. He was beautiful, dark, mysterious. He could have been one of the men in the hotel photographs from long ago. She realized then with a faint jolt of surprise that she trusted him more at that moment, than anyone else.

And just when had that happened? Overnight maybe? Under the spell of Wolfe Creek's ardent moon? It had certainly been capable of stranger things. At some point Koda Wolfe had stopped being just an acquaintance and had begun to be something else all together.

He bent slightly, his black eyes fixed on hers. She didn't want to think, didn't want to feel. She just wanted to fall into this moment and let it carry her away like the rush of a swollen river.

When his lips touched hers, they were warm and wet. Salty. She could feel an urgency there, yet he moved deliberately slow, as if not wanting to scare her. She responded by opening her mouth and touching her tongue to his. Everything inside her coiled. She was no longer full of pain, but of a longing so powerful that it threatened to turn her inside out. And she welcomed it.

His strong hands pressed into her back, bringing her

even closer. Her breasts rubbed against his chest, her nipples hard and sensitive through her thin cotton bra. A wild pulse beat at the hollow of her throat, making her light-headed.

And then a sound. A footstep behind them that coaxed a moan from the old hardwood floor. Maggie sucked in a breath and Koda broke the kiss.

She turned to see Zane standing in the archway. His eyes glittered, his lips curled into a grin.

"I thought you told me to stay away from her, brother," he said. "Now I see why."

Koda sat at his desk, looking at the photographs in Candi's file for the hundredth time. Bruises, cuts, the broken screen door, the shattered lamp. *Candace Tina Brooks,* said the tidy label on the side. So formal, so cold.

Exhausted, he leaned back and rubbed his face with both hands.

It was Sunday morning and the substation was so quiet, he could hear a pin drop. He was the only deputy on duty, which wasn't unusual. But the eerie silence was. Even the phone that usually rang off the hook on the weekends was still. The only sound that was keeping him from going completely nuts was the occasional crackly voice coming through the radio in the corner. But even that was quieter than normal.

Looking at the desk again, he poked at the lighter that had been sitting there for the last few days. It seemed ridiculously out of place next to the files and sticky notes that scattered Koda's work surface. Its gaudiness reminded him of Zane as a teenager, trying so hard to be tough, and eventually, after a lot of adolescent effort, succeeding.

Koda flicked it until it spun in a blur of gold. He didn't know why he hadn't given it back yet. Busy, he guessed. With everything going on, ensuring that his brother's smoking habit went uninterrupted hadn't been a priority. Zane must have left it at Candi's during one of their jaunts. But it was strange that he hadn't mentioned how it was missing, even in passing. He loved that stupid thing.

Koda's cell phone rang, making him jump.

"Wolfe," he barked into the phone, suddenly cranky.

"Koda, it's McCay."

Alan McCay was an OSP trooper, who'd also been a buddy since high school. He was one of the lead investigators on the Aimee Styles case, and despite what Maggie thought, had been working himself to the bone for the last twelve months.

Koda sat forward and switched the phone to his other ear. "Hey. I know you're running ragged. How's it going?" An avid outdoorsman, it was usually Alan who had the knowledge and expertise to lead the search parties when someone went missing on the mountain. More often than not, he was stretched paper-thin. It was a relentless, exhausting job. When Koda saw him these days, he looked worn around the edges, always of the verge of either snapping, or falling asleep in his chair.

"It's going," Alan said. "It's going like you wouldn't fucking believe."

He had a mouth like a trucker. It was one of his endearing traits, depending on who you were talking to. He never said *Good morning.* Instead, it was usually *Good fucking morning,* with an emphasis on *fucking.*

"Yeah?" Koda grinned, glad to hear his friend's voice.

"I'm right around the corner. Wanted to see if you could use a coffee."

"Always."

"Copy that. Be there in five."

When he walked in the door a few minutes later, he carried a steaming cup and shoved it at Koda unceremoniously.

"Thanks." Koda wiped a few drops from the lid and motioned for him to sit.

"Can't stay," Alan said, leaning against Koda's desk. His short brown hair was a little messy. His face, more tan than usual. He looked fit in his dark navy uniform, like he'd been working out. But all the mountain work probably accounted for that. "I heard about Candi. Saw her last week. Stopped in the café to grab a quick bite. Jesus. Is she okay?"

"She'll be fine," Koda said, leaning back in his chair. "It could have been worse."

"Well, yeah. I guess if she was dead, it could have been," he said. "I asked her out again, you know. Turned me down cold. Guess she's still into your brother. I gotta tell you, I don't know what the fuck she sees in him."

Koda felt a familiar rush of protectiveness for Zane. Because this was Alan, he bit his tongue. But most people who were stupid enough to say anything about his brother in person, would have ended up with a fist in the face.

"How are *you?*" Alan asked, as if sensing he'd over-stepped a bit. "I hear you're getting hot and heavy with the Sullivan girl. That true?"

Koda scratched his jaw. He'd expected word would spread, but it was still faster than usual. Zane had been furious last night, and even though Koda didn't believe in all that vengeful mountain-man bullshit, he could understand where his little brother was coming from. He knew without question that it wasn't a good idea to be fanning the flames with Maggie Sullivan. He'd certainly never intended for this to happen. But the truth was, he hadn't been able to keep his hands off her. There was something about Maggie. Something that, despite the stubborn tilt to her chin, was incredibly fragile. And that was something he'd always been the worst kind of sucker for.

"I don't know that hot and heavy is how I'd put it." Actually, it kind of was, but Alan didn't need to know that. "She came here looking for some answers and I've agreed to help as much as I can. Within reason."

"Help *with* or with*out* her panties on?"

"Don't be a dick."

Alan chuckled. "I can respect that. I can. Just don't give up any of our sensitive info. The top-secret shit."

"As far as I know we don't have any info, so that shouldn't be a problem."

"That's where you're wrong, my brother in blue. Er… brown."

Ignoring the deputy jab, Koda sat forward.

"What's going on?"

Alan shook his head. "One year. An entire fucking year and not a single goddamn clue. As far as anyone around here can tell, Aimee Styles disappears into thin air. Not a scream, not a witness, not a fucking clue. Am I right?"

"Right."

"And then all of a sudden, one year to the day, to the goddamn *day,* we got something. *Bam.* Out of the blue."

Koda's pulse picked up, and all of a sudden the room

felt hot.

"What do you have?"

"Yesterday a hunter stumbled across something. Over by the stream that runs down from Pikes Peak. He saw something in the bushes. Something pink."

"What?"

"A fucking *bra*. Victoria's Secret. The fancy kind."

Victoria's Secret. The kind Aimee wore. "Holy shit. What size?"

"Thirty-six B."

"Her size?"

"Her fucking size, man."

They were quiet for a minute. A year was a long time to go without any clues. Now, they had something. Even if it was something small, it was still something.

"What now?" Koda asked.

"Now we're bringing in cadaver dogs."

Koda sighed inwardly. Of course that would be the next step. He knew this, just like he knew the chances of Aimee being found alive were probably less than zero. Still, the knowledge made him a little nauseous. He'd have to tell Maggie. If she didn't already know.

Alan slapped the desk. "Well, I gotta go, man. Just wanted to keep you in the loop. I realize you guys are the last to hear down there."

That was the understatement of the century. The top brass at OSP and the FBI had a way of treating the Deep Water County Sheriff's Department like a bothersome younger sibling.

"I appreciate it, Alan. Thanks."

"No problem, brother. And let's grab lunch pretty soon,

okay?"

"Yeah. Just let me know when and I'm there."

"Things are going to be bat-shit crazy around here for the next few days. But after that, definitely."

"Sure."

Koda watched him walk out the door and climb into his cruiser.

One year. One year with nothing, and now this. And on the anniversary of her disappearance. Coincidence? Right now it was impossible to tell if the bra was found by sheer luck, or if it was placed there in order to be found.

Again, his stomach turned. Just when he'd thought this case couldn't get any more bizarre.

Needing some air, he grabbed his jacket and keys. But froze dead in his tracks before he'd even reached the door.

The bastard took my bra, Candi had said.

Chapter Fifteen

"That's so sweet. You can just put them over there." Candi eased herself onto the couch. "Yellow's my favorite. How'd you know?"

Maggie smiled and set the small vase of roses on the dining room table. "Ara told me. I was going to get pink. I'm glad I asked."

Candi grimaced. "I hate pink."

She looked much better today. She'd ended up staying in the hospital a few nights and was released yesterday. The swelling in her face had gone down significantly and the bruises seemed to be healing well. They'd gone from a deep black and blue, to tinged with lime green. But she still looked beautiful.

This morning her face was scrubbed clean, and small diamond studs adorned each earlobe. They sparkled in the shaft of sunlight she sat in.

"Like my new setup?" She nodded toward the front

door where two shiny dead bolts had just been installed. "The landlord did it. Makes me feel better."

Maggie glanced out the window where a sheriff's cruiser sat. "I see you're being watched, too."

"That was Koda's doing. I don't like it. Feels like I'm being stalked, but he insisted. At least the deputy doesn't stay. They don't have the manpower for that. He just shows up every now and then to make sure I'm not dead. Plus, Zane is making a damn nuisance of himself already. Won't leave me alone."

"At least that's a good problem to have, right? Surrounded by gorgeous men all day."

Candi seemed to consider this and nodded happily. "So, tell me," she said after a minute, "how are you doing? I know it must have been hard."

At that, Maggie's knees felt weak and she sat. Koda had been the one to tell her that Aimee's bra had been found in a remote part of the wilderness a few days before. But she'd seen it on the news not long after. The reporters had been all over it, blood thirsty and hoping for a body. But none had materialized, and in the last twenty-four hours, they seemed to have lost interest.

"It is," Maggie said. "It's horrible to think how it got there. That at some point it was actually ripped off her." She paused, composing herself. "But then again, it's a clue. And I'm glad about that. It's something that might eventually lead us to her killer. Or her."

Candi frowned. "True."

"But Koda…he's avoiding me now. I think he's afraid I'm going to want to go hunting around up there by myself."

"Are you?"

Maggie shook her head. "I don't know. Yes. I guess if I'm being honest, yes. But I don't want to go alone."

"Honey, don't take this the wrong way, but those cops have been searching up there on horses, with bloodhounds. I don't know that you'd find anything they haven't."

"You sound like my mother. She said the same thing."

"I'm sorry."

"No, it's okay. You're right. So is she. I doubt we'd find anything either. It doesn't make any sense, but it's the same reason I wanted to come here. I needed to see for myself. Sitting around not doing anything can drive you crazy."

Candi took this in with an empathetic look on her face. She had a way of making Maggie feel validated, which meant a lot.

"Do what you have to do," Candi said. "If you're gonna go, Koda is the one to take you. He knows that mountain like the back of his hand."

"Do you think he would?"

"I've seen the way he looks at you. If I know him, all you'll have to do is bat those big green eyes and the rest will be history."

Maggie doubted this. She'd never batted her eyes in her life. At least not since she'd been about six years old. Still, she was intrigued by the idea that using her female charms might work on a man like Koda Wolfe.

"Besides," Candi said. "He wants to find out what happened, too. This case has consumed him. It really has."

Maggie felt a twinge of guilt over what she'd said that night in front of the Inn. That the police weren't doing enough to find Aimee. She'd known when she'd said it that it wasn't really true. She'd spoken out of frustration and pain.

Now, sitting here talking to Candi, whose bruises bloomed over her delicate white skin, she was ashamed of herself. Countless men and women had combed a dangerous, remote part of the mountainside just a few days ago, putting their own lives at risk, hoping to find Aimee or at the very least, find out what happened to her. Koda was no exception.

"I know," Maggie said.

"Hey. Look at me." Candi's expression was tender. "I mean it. Do what you need to do. Go look for her if that's what's going to give you peace. Koda won't let you go alone."

Maggie nodded, grateful.

They were quiet for a minute, before Candi grinned and slapped her knee. "Hey! I almost forgot to tell you. I'm getting a dog."

"Oh yeah? What kind?"

"The ferocious kind." She reached over to grab her cell. "I'm adopting him from the shelter in Splendor. Here's a picture."

Maggie took the phone, expecting a Rottweiler type, or a pit-bull mix of some kind. Something thick and formidable. Instead, the photo was dominated by big brown eyes, floppy ears, and a wide, slobbery mouth.

"His name is Bart," Candi said, obviously proud.

"Aww! He's adorable. Is he…supposed to be aggressive?" She couldn't fathom this dog with the friendly, goofy face ever taking exception to anyone, much less an intruder.

Taking the phone back, Candi beamed like a new mother. "I don't think he's aggressive, really. But his foster parents say he's a good guard dog and very loyal. I explained what happened to me and they said he would have been a deterrent." She tucked the phone back in her purse. "I've always wanted a dog, but never got around to getting one. Now I have an excuse."

Maggie felt an unexpected rush of affection for this woman, this ex-stripper and practical stranger, who had worked her way into her heart in just a matter of days. "I'm so happy for you," she said. "I can't wait to meet him."

Koda rolled his eyes, exasperated. He'd known this had been coming, but he hadn't expected her to be so damn relentless.

He turned his back on her now, ready to walk out the door, exactly the way he'd come in just five minutes before.

"Wait." She put a hand on his arm. "Will you just hear me out?"

"Why? This is ridiculous."

"It's not!"

He looked down at her hand on his biceps, and she dropped it, coloring.

"It's not ridiculous," she said again, this time softer.

"Maggie," he said, turning. "Trained professionals spent three days looking up there. They didn't find shit. They had dogs, a helicopter, horses. They covered every square inch, I can promise you that."

"I know." Her eyes were wide, pleading. "And I know I'm asking a lot. But I'm also asking you to understand. I need this."

He shook his head. "Crazy. This is *craziness*. What are you suggesting? Camping out? The temperatures are near freezing at night. There are bears, cougars."

"You're just trying to scare me. I know you're not worried about that."

"No. But I was raised here. You weren't. And I don't want to be stuck up there when you end up changing your mind and want to hike out in the middle of the night."

"Will you give me a little credit? I'm not that much of a pansy."

He considered this. Actually, he didn't doubt she'd stick it out up there. And that's what worried him. What in Christ's name was he getting himself into?

"I'd be so grateful," she said, her voice touching something deep inside of him. She stepped closer and he caught her scent. Her lips curved just slightly, as if she knew instinctively what kind of power she had over him.

He shook his head again, feeling his resolve weaken.

"But the truth is," she continued,"I'm going with, or without you."

Clenching his jaw, he thought about telling her to go ahead. See how far she got. He was tired and antsy. And this whole conversation wasn't helping his mood any.

Then she looked up. Her eyes were the exact color of the ponderosa pines that stood at the edge of town. And all of a sudden, he couldn't find it within himself to say no.

Throwing his head back, he sighed. "Shiiit."

She blinked, looking proud of herself. And a little surprised.

"I'll pick you up in the morning," he mumbled. "Be ready at six."

Maggie had waited.

The attendant hadn't said much, but had seemed normal

enough, despite the creepy surroundings. "Where ya'll headed?" he'd asked.

"San Francisco. A girls' weekend."

He'd nodded, as if all too familiar with people passing through on their way to more appealing destinations.

Maggie paced the aisles of junk food, catching his eye every now and then, and smiling.

Aimee had been sick a few days ago. Maybe she was having a hard time again. All the chips and soda probably didn't help. But the minutes had stretched into five. And then ten.

She'd walked over to the bathroom door and knocked. "Still alive in there?" Nothing. Just the constant buzzing of the neon beer sign in the window. She'd knocked again, this time louder. More insistent. "Aimee?"

Maggie sat now in the passenger seat of Koda's truck, remembering. They'd been driving for almost half an hour and had just turned off onto a narrow gravel road, which wound up the mountainside like a boa constrictor. She watched the trees swoosh past and held her breath every time a chipmunk scurried into the truck's path.

To their right, Pikes Peak rose up like a giant prehistoric thing, its crags dwarfing them in shadow. To their left was a dramatic drop-off at least two hundred feet, if not more. Maggie had always been afraid of heights, and was grateful for the memories of that night, if only to keep her occupied with thoughts other than the truck careening over the edge.

Koda glanced over. "You okay?"

"Yeah. Just thinking."

"About?"

"Aimee, mostly. But also the fact that I hate this road."

He grinned. "You don't trust my driving?"

"I don't trust the stability of this mountainside."

"I think we'll be all right."

She looked back out the window. It really was breath-taking. Of course there were beautiful mountains up north, too. But living in Portland, they always seemed so far away. She didn't get out of the city much, so even though she was an Oregonian at heart, all of this was new territory.

The sun was finally waking up and lighting the sky in a mixture of purple and orange that reminded her of swirled ice cream. They were above the fog, and the vastness of the mountain range stretched as far as she could see. It was as if she were peering over the wing of an airplane.

And still, they kept climbing. The truck barreled around every curve while kicking gravel up behind them and making Maggie clutch her seat with both hands.

"We're almost there," Koda said. "We'll leave the truck and hike in the rest of the way."

"Oh. Yeah, okay."

She'd known there would be hiking involved, and had been lucky enough to fit into a pair of Candi's old boots. She wiggled her toes. Her feet were warm and toasty now, but they wouldn't be in an hour or so.

All the other camping stuff was Koda's. The tent, sleeping bags, backpacks. He was more than prepared, and she had a sneaking suspicion that he welcomed the chance to put all this alpha-male stuff to good use.

A serious-looking rifle hung behind her in the window

and she knew it would be coming along as well. She'd never handled a gun before, and just knowing it was there made her nervous.

They turned another corner and Koda finally pulled over. Prickly branches and twigs brushed against Maggie's door, and a cloud of dust rose up as they came to a stop.

He turned off the engine and looked over, his dark eyes unreadable.

"Here we go," he said.

Chapter Sixteen

Koda hiked up the gradual incline, mindful all the while of Maggie trudging along behind. Her breathing was fairly heavy and so were her steps. He knew she wasn't used to this kind of exertion, but she didn't complain. Every now and then he'd look back. She'd be deep in thought, studying the ground in front of her like it was going to open up and swallow her whole.

"You doing okay?" he asked.

"Yup." She smiled. "How much farther?"

"Not far now." They'd been walking for forty-five minutes, and it was cold. Really cold. The mountain was steep and treacherous. Hard to hike in the best conditions. Much harder when your feet and hands were numb.

He looked around and took a deep breath. What he'd said to Maggie earlier was true. He was used to the outdoors. To this mountain in particular. He and Zane had camped here countless times as teenagers. Ara had always worried,

sending them with too much food and making them promise to be careful. It was a popular area for local hunters and
fisherman because the mountain came to a plateau not far
from where he and Maggie were now. There was a narrow
meadow there that was alive in the spring with deer, rabbits
and wildflowers. Around it snaked a stream that eventually
turned into a river, which led all the way to the mouth of the
Pacific Ocean.

Koda and Zane were familiar with every inch of this area,
and had spent some of their best boyhood days up here. He
felt much more comfortable here, than in the woods around
Wolfe Creek. He hated those. Always had.

"Ouch!"

Koda turned to see Maggie hopping on one foot and
reached out to steady her. "What happened?"

"Twisted my ankle. Crap!"

She leaned into him and all of a sudden, the chill of the
air was forgotten. She was warm and pliant, her body yield-
ing against his. He caught the scent of her hair. Soapy, clean.
No fuss. Her curls were tied into a ponytail and her face was
flushed with the cold.

"Am I going to have to carry you out, young lassie?"

She laughed. "*No*. I think I can manage."

He adjusted the pack on his shoulder and stepped away.
The thought of picking her up was something he could get
used to. Picking her up and carrying her to his bed, was
more like it. He hadn't touched her since the morning they'd
kissed, but that one brief encounter had left him wanting
more. Much more.

"Ready?"

She kept her eyes down and fidgeted with her gloves.

"Ready."

By the time they got to the meadow, it was well after nine. Maggie sat on a fallen log and wriggled out of her pack. "I'm starving," she said. "I don't think I've ever been this hungry in my life."

Koda took his own pack off, unzipped it, and handed her a granola bar. "It's the hiking. We're gonna make a mountain woman out of you yet."

She unwrapped it and took a bite. "I don't know. I feel like a fish out of water up here."

"I think you're doing great. Maybe this is where you were meant to be."

Her cheeks were rosy, her freckles standing out against her fair skin. The cold suited her.

He smiled, but she was suddenly wistful. Lowering the granola bar into her lap, she looked around.

"I can't stop thinking about her," she said. "I keep wondering if he brought her up here. If he hurt her here."

"Don't do that to yourself, Maggie."

"I know it's not helping. But that's been the hardest part. Wondering what happened and filling in the blanks myself."

Koda knelt in the dirt, elbows on his knees. "Are you really sure you want to do this? It's not going to be easy. Are you sure it's going to give you some peace, or is it going to make things worse?"

She twisted the wrapper between her fingers. "I need this. I know it's going to be hard. But everything has been so far. I think it'll give me a little peace, yes. That's what I'm hoping for anyway."

He nodded and slung the rifle over his shoulder. "Okay. Let's get going, then.

"*Aimee, stop fooling around. You're scaring me.*" *Maggie knocked louder, this time drawing the attention of the clerk.*

"*Everything okay?*"

Maggie's teeth had begun to chatter. She had a bad feeling.

"*I don't know. She's not answering. Do you have a key?*"

"*Right here.*" *After a few seconds of fumbling, he unlocked the door.*

They'd been met with a blast of cold air. The small window above the toilet was wide open. Water dripped from the faucet into the rusted sink.

Aimee was gone.

"*Aimee? Aimee!*"

"*Maybe she went outside while your car was filling up,*" *the clerk had said.*

Maggie pushed past him and ran down the candy-bar aisle. Something was wrong. Something was really, really wrong.

She hit the front door and immediately saw the car was empty.

She'd stood in the parking lot and turned around, scanning the darkness for Aimee. Maybe she'd gotten sick? Maybe she'd needed some air? But nothing was making any sense.

The clerk had come up behind her. "Did you two have a fight?"

Maggie choked back a sob. She looked at her watch. They'd been here for close to half an hour now. "No, we didn't have a fight."

"*Okay. Calm down. She probably just…*" *But he never finished his sentence. She probably just what? She probably just walked off into the woods by herself in a strange town in the middle of the night?*

Maggie looked around, panicked. "I'm sorry. But this isn't like her. Can you call the police?"

"Don't you think we should look first?"

"No!" She'd been close to losing it. "I think we should call the police."

He dialed 911 and they were told to wait for a deputy.

Maggie began walking in big, sweeping circles, calling Aimee's name every few seconds. Her voice echoed into the night, but no one answered.

It had taken twenty minutes for the first deputy to arrive; a portly, middle-aged man who didn't seem very concerned. He'd asked all kinds of questions. Did Aimee use drugs? Was she unhappy? Had they had a disagreement? Maggie shook her head to all of them.

"She's only been gone an hour. I'm sure she'll turn up," he'd said.

But an hour had stretched into two. And then Maggie had to make the call to Aimee's parents. They'd been scared to death, of course. But they'd also tried to reassure her. "It's not your fault," they'd said. "We're on our way."

But by four o'clock in the morning, Trooper McCay had been assigned to Maggie. He stood before her looking stiff and formal.

"What happened to her?" she'd asked.

"I don't know." He put a hand on her arm. "But we're going to find out, okay?"

Maggie walked methodically now through the underbrush of the forest on the outskirts of the meadow. Koda was only about thirty feet away. Every now and then a twig would snap, and she'd look up to see him, a reassuring presence in the otherwise disturbing afternoon.

Then her gaze would fall again, moving over the ground just like he'd taught her. But her thoughts were far away. They belonged, like they did most of the time, to that night. Over and over again, the movie would play in her head. The horror movie with an ending that left everyone hanging.

For the last several hours, she'd walked and looked. Walked and looked. Her feet were cold; her legs ached. She wondered what it must have been like for Koda's ancestors here. How hard it must have been. If the weather didn't kill them, sickness would. She remembered the wedding picture hanging above the staircase at the Inn. She thought about the couple whose union had sparked such controversy, such hatred between two sets of families. And she thought about the so-called curse which followed them into the next century. *Lupus. Wolves.* One in the same? Had Wolfe Creek ever been a place of happiness? Or was it destined to be marked by tragedy and loss?

She'd lain awake the last few nights thinking about the story Koda had told her. And she'd finally decided that this legend, this incredibly tall tale, was simply a way of explaining away such tragedy. Of giving it some magical quality that it never would have had otherwise. Werewolves were something out of a mythical fairy tale. Lupus was a horrific reality.

Maggie glanced at her watch. 4:35. The sun would be setting soon, bringing dusk with it. They'd walked painstakingly around the area where the bra had been found. All day and they'd seen nothing else.

She stopped and looked around. The air was cold on her cheeks, numbing them to perfection. It was a constant reminder of that night. *Everything* was a reminder of that night. The cold, the fog, the darkness.

Koda walked up from behind and she blinked.

"Think it's time to knock off for today," he said.

"Okay."

He touched the small of her back. When she leaned into him, he slid his hands up to massage her shoulders. "You all right?"

She nodded, temporarily speechless. Even though this was probably the hardest thing she'd ever done, she was grateful that Koda had brought her here. Thankful for his unexpected friendship in the midst of such pain.

Turning, she smiled. Just the simple act briefly lifted her spirits. "Thank you," she said. "Thank you so much."

He looked thoughtful. Studying her in such a way that made her want to reach up and touch his face. His black hair moved in the light breeze, making it curve inward at the nape of his neck. For another few seconds they stood there, neither one looking away.

And then the last of the sun sank behind the violet mountaintops. His jaw twitched and he took a step back, as if he were afraid of what he might do next.

"I'd better get the tent set up," he said. "It'll be cold tonight."

Chapter Seventeen

The fire crackled and hissed, its sparks rising into the darkness to float away like tiny orange stars in the night.

Maggie scooted close, exhausted, but content. They'd had tomato soup with saltines for dinner, and she didn't think anything had ever tasted so good. For dessert, Koda brought out a giant Hershey bar and split it in half.

Maggie nibbled on a corner. "My *favorite*. How'd you know?"

"I didn't. Aunt A always keeps a box of candy bars in her cupboard. I raided it before we left."

"A woman after my own heart."

"It's ridiculous. We used to walk around with constant stomach aches when we were kids."

Maggie watched the campfire dance, felt its heat on her face. The smell brought back memories of her dad taking her camping when she was little. She'd almost forgotten there had been a time when she'd liked the woods.

"You wouldn't want to see my thighs if I had twenty-four-hour access to a box of chocolate," she said.

"Oh, I don't know. You could probably twist my arm."

She laughed, but something deep inside fluttered at the words. "How do you stay looking so…" *Perfect, gorgeous, lickable…* "healthy?" she asked, managing to keep her eyes locked on his face and not his body, where they really wanted to be.

"Oh, you know." Flexing, he kissed a biceps. "I lift."

"Yeah?"

"No." He took another bite of chocolate. "I'm too lazy. I do hike a lot, though. Ara made sure we grew up to appreciate the outdoors. Kind of had to, living up here."

Maggie smiled. "Sounds like you and Zane had good childhoods."

"We did. I don't know what we would have done without A. Most likely would have been farmed out by the state. Foster home after foster home. That's what happens."

"Candi said you were babies when you came to live there?"

He nodded, staring into the fire.

"What happened to your parents?" It was direct, but at this point Maggie didn't know any other way to be.

"My mother died during childbirth with Zane. My father was sick. He passed away a few months after she did."

Maggie swallowed the hard, uncomfortable lump in her throat. She could almost see them as babies, dealt such a cruel hand at such a tender age. And she suddenly wanted to hug Ara. Not just hug her, but hold on to her like a little kid might. Around the middle for dear life. "I'm so sorry," she finally said.

He shrugged. "It is what it is. We got lucky with A, for sure. She's my mother's sister. She raised us the best way she could, never let us forget our parents. We grew up hearing stories, seeing pictures. She did a good job."

"She did." *That's an understatement*, Maggie thought, watching the man sitting across from her. *She did an amazing job.* "So you came to live with her, and then Candi did, too."

"Yeah. Candi came when she was thirteen. She was a mess. Would have broken your heart. But she's tough. She rose above it, and A turned out to be the mother she never had. Taught her almost everything she knows."

"And you and Zane grew to be family, too."

He smiled and looked up. "I guess you could say that. I grew to be family. Zane grew to be something else."

Maggie poked at the fire with a stick, sending fresh sparks into the air. "She told me how she feels about him. Does he feel the same?"

"Their relationship is complicated. They're very passionate, but you probably guessed that. They fight a lot. But they make up a lot, too."

Maggie flushed. Hearing him talk about sex was having an embarrassing effect. All of a sudden, she was warmer than she should have been. She shifted and unzipped her fleece a little.

"It must have been hard on Ara," she said, eager to change the subject. "Raising three kids on her own. Was it always just her? Was there ever anyone else?"

"Pretty much. No husband. No man, other than Jim, and he's just a friend. He's been working for her for a long time. He never helped out with us directly, but he's kept the place afloat for years. Anything goes wrong, he fixes it.

There's nothing the man can't do. Plumbing, electricity, carpentry, you name it. If it weren't for him, she wouldn't have been able to keep the Inn. My parents left it to her in their will, and I know there have been times when she's wanted to do other things, travel, explore. But she has a deep sense of loyalty. I think she feels she'd be letting them down if she ever left." He cocked his head to the side, cracking his neck. "Anyway, Jim's been a godsend."

"I've seen him working around the yard. I've never talked to him, though."

"Don't expect to. He's really shy. I grew up with the guy, and I can count the number of conversations I've had with him on both hands."

"The strong, silent type."

"Yeah, and he's crazy smart. My aunt has a lot of respect for him, and it's not just because he's been there for so long. She knows him better than anyone in Wolfe Creek."

"I'm glad she has someone. Something about her being there by herself makes me sad."

"Me, too," he said.

They grew quiet, staring into the fire that crackled with a little less vitality now. Every few minutes an owl would hoot from somewhere in the canopy of evergreen branches above.

When Maggie looked up, Koda was watching her.

"What?"

His expression was unreadable. The firelight played over his face, making his eyes look even darker than before.

"Nothing," he finally said, getting up and brushing off his jeans. "I'm tired. Gonna go to bed."

Maggie glanced at the tent behind her. Army green and no frills. She knew the sleeping bags that waited inside were equally simple. But quite frankly, she didn't think she'd ever seen anything so suggestive. She'd known that they'd be sleeping next to each other of course, but hadn't let herself think about what that might mean. Until now.

She looked up at Koda, who stepped over the log she was sitting on without a second glance.

"What about the fire?" she asked.

"Let it burn. It won't hurt anything and the extra heat will come in handy for a while."

He picked up the battery-powered lantern and unzipped the tent, crouching low to step inside. Maggie eyed the yawning black mouth of the forest, which seemed somehow closer than before.

"Wait for me." She scrambled off the log and climbed into the tent just in time to see him peeling off his gray thermal shirt. The lantern light illuminated his smooth, hard chest, where his nipples puckered like small brown stones. Maggie looked away.

"Oh...uh..." She stood up, squashing her head into the top of the tent. "Aren't you going to be cold?"

"I can't sleep with clothes on."

"Oh." She sat down awkwardly, still unable to look at him.

Tossing the shirt in the corner, he lay down and pulled the sleeping bag over his chest.

"It's okay," he said. "I won't bite."

Maggie laughed a little too quickly. It was like she'd never slept next to a smoking-hot, naked sheriff's deputy before.

"Are you going to keep that jacket on?" He watched her with one arm crooked under his head, obviously amused.

"No. I... No."

"I won't look. Promise."

He turned away. She waited for a second, then hesitantly unzipped her jacket. Outside the tent, the fire was dying to embers, but she could still feel its lingering heat on her skin. She fished around in her pack for the old college T-shirt and yoga pants she'd brought as pajamas and glanced at Koda again, making sure he wasn't looking.

Heart pounding, she wrestled out of her jeans and top, almost falling onto her face more than once. Only when she was tucked securely into her sleeping bag, pj's and all, did she take her bra off through the armhole of her shirt. She stuffed it into her pack and wriggled into the comforting down like a baby chick.

"Okay. All done. You can look now."

Smiling, he rolled over and propped his head on his hand. "I thought you might have brought another parka to change into."

She grinned. The sleeping bag was pulled strategically to her chin. For all he knew, she could be naked, too. The thought teased her senses. Made her warm in places she'd forgotten existed.

Her gaze dropped to his shoulders, which were angular and strong. Tawny skin stretched over lean muscle and sinew. And then she looked away. What was wrong with her? The air between them was charged. She shifted in her sleeping bag, aware of a mild throbbing between her legs. It was as if someone else were lying here next to this man. Someone with more of a right to. A woman who was more feminine and experienced. Not skinny little Margaret Sullivan with the wiry hair and crazy freckles. She was a girl. Maybe always would be. Not a woman. And she had no idea what to do with this situation that had presented itself like something out of a high school fantasy.

She closed her eyes for a second, heady with the scent of the man beside her, of the forest, of the campfire. She was conflicted. She was supposed to hate this place. Was supposed to hate everything about it. And yet, she didn't. Part of her wanted to hate it, but she couldn't quite muster the effort anymore. It was growing on her. *He* was growing on her, and had been since the day he'd walked through the doors of the Arrowhead Café two weeks ago.

"Hey," he said, his voice low.

She opened her eyes to see him staring at her.

"What?" Instinctively she knew something was about to happen between them. He was too quiet. Too intent.

He reached out to smooth her hair away from her forehead. His hand was warm and rough on her skin.

"I'm proud of you," he said.

She took him in. The curve of his mouth, his impossibly long eyelashes, the steady pulse at the base of his neck.

"Proud? Why?"

"You're very brave. But you have to know that."

He took his hand away, and she wanted to cry out. Wanted to beg him to put it back. But she just lay there.

"I'm not," she said. "I'm a coward."

"Why would you say that?"

"I never should have left that night. I never should have left without her."

"That's not realistic and you know it. There was nothing you could have done here."

Maggie's throat ached. She studied the top of the tent, the clean, crisp lines of it. "She asked me never to leave her."

She looked at Koda, trying to keep her voice steady. "In the car on the way down. She said it out of the blue."

Frowning, he waited for her to go on.

"And I did leave. When she needed me most, I went back home." Her eyes filled then. "I love that you say I'm brave. I want to be, but I'm not. I'm just not."

He ran his knuckles down her cheek. "But you came back. Not many people would, and you did."

"Are we ever going to find her?"

"I don't know," he said. "I hope we do. Her family deserves closure. You do, too."

"I don't know what I deserve. Why her? Why her and not me?"

"I don't think there has to be a reason. I think she was the one who went to use the bathroom at that exact moment, and you didn't. I think it's just that simple. You can't blame yourself."

"I know," she said. "I know it doesn't make any sense to feel that way. But deep down, I can't help it."

"You experienced a major trauma, Maggie. Even though you escaped without being hurt, doesn't make it any less traumatic. You need to give yourself time to heal. You need to give yourself *permission* to heal. Stop punishing yourself for things that were out of your control. What happened to Aimee was the fault of whatever sick bastard took her. Not yours. Not anyone else's."

His face was drawn, his brows furrowed.

"How'd you get to be so smart?"

"I've been a cop for a while." He smiled, relaxing a little. "They train you for this stuff."

And then, before she had time to wonder whether or

not it was a good idea, she leaned forward and kissed him. A light kiss on the side of the mouth, lingering there for just a second. Long enough to taste him. And then she pulled away, shaking her head. This would complicate things. A lot. And maybe things didn't need to get any more complicated, no matter how much she wanted more of Koda Wolfe. *Sensible Maggie,* she could almost hear Aimee say. *What a buzz kill.*

"I'm sorry. I'm—"

Before she could finish, he was kissing her back, pressing his heavy body against hers through the sleeping bag. Slowly, she wrapped her arms around his neck, basking in the feel of his hair against her bare skin. He was a good kisser. Slow, confident. He coaxed her mouth open and touched his tongue to hers.

He kissed her like that for a minute, maybe two, long enough for her to want to shed the sleeping bag completely. She wasn't cold anymore. Far from it.

When he pulled away, she was breathing hard.

"Why would you be sorry for kissing me?" he asked, his voice husky.

"It might change things… I didn't know if you'd want to again."

He shoved a hand through his hair, making it stand straight up. "Are you kidding? It's all I've been thinking about for the last seventy-two hours."

"Really?"

He bent and pressed his lips to her neck. "Really."

She exhaled slowly as he began moving south, kissing the hollow of her throat and then her collarbone, moving his lips in such a way as to coax muffled sounds from her.

He stretched the neck of her T-shirt a little and touched his open mouth to just above her breasts. Gasping, she arched her back.

"You know, I wouldn't want to pressure a lady," he said. "But I might be able to get to second base without this in the way."

It was dim in the tent, but she could make out the expression on his face and it gave her butterflies. He was fantastically gorgeous. And he wanted *her.*

Reaching down, she pulled her T-shirt over her head and tossed it in the corner. The night air was chilly on her exposed skin, but she barely noticed.

He dipped his head and breathed softly over one breast. She closed her eyes, feeling her nipple grow hard in response. Then he breathed over the other, before teasing it with his tongue and drawing it into his mouth. She moaned, wanting more. Needing more.

Outside the tent, a coyote yipped. Another answered not far away. Mates, maybe. Calling to each other from across the darkness.

Koda unzipped the sleeping bag down to her hips. She ran her hands along his lean, muscled back, which was warm and smooth as beach glass. He sucked in a breath as her fingers played across his rib cage.

Groaning, he pulled away. "I think we might be headed toward more than second base here."

She lifted her head off the camp pillow and kissed his neck. "I'm okay with a home run if you are." And there she was again. That woman Maggie didn't recognize as herself. The one about to have sex with someone she'd only known a few weeks. That Maggie was naked from the waist up, huddled in a tent on the side of a cold, dark mountain.

Koda unzipped his sleeping bag and held it open. "Come here," he said.

Maggie stared at him, his face bathed in shadow, his body taking the shape of something out of her dreams. Strong, lithe, surreal.

She wriggled out of her yoga pants and tossed them in the corner with her shirt where they seemed destined to be. Shivering with anticipation, she crawled in next to him, still unable to believe what she was doing. It had been so long since she'd been lost in anything other than misery, that she was tumbling now, headfirst into this decision, and toward this man who was waiting to catch her with his arms open wide. Whether it was right or wrong, she no longer cared.

She lay down next to him and had to clamp her jaw together to keep her teeth from chattering.

"Cold?" he murmured against her temple.

"No. Just nervous." That was true. She was hyperaware of every single inch of his skin. The smooth, bare chest, the muscled thigh sprinkled with rough hair, the erection that was hot and hard against her hip. He smelled so good, almost like the mountains themselves. Fresh and clean. And suddenly she had a vision of what it would have been like a hundred and fifty years ago. Not in a tent, but inside a narrow dome made of sun bleached animal skin. Lying on fur, maybe wolf, maybe coyote. Koda's hair would have been long, like Zane's, and smelling like rainwater. Maybe he would have spoken to her in his Native tongue. Erotic and low, his voice mingling with the sounds of the woods around them, alive with the rustling of animals and birds.

Maggie closed her eyes, seeing this just as clearly as she

felt his breath on her jaw now.

He moved his hand down her side, his fingers tickling the sensitive skin of her belly, and then her bikini line.

"You're beautiful, Maggie," he said, his voice almost lost in the tangles of her hair.

She caught her breath. He touched the inside of her thigh, resting his hand there until she arched her hips and shifted toward him.

"Please," she whispered.

Slowly, agonizingly his fingers finally found her, slick and wet. She whimpered as he moved them over her swollen bud again and again, teasing her, bringing her close to the edge, but not over. Not quite yet.

She opened her legs wider. He kissed her neck, bit her earlobe, then slipped a finger inside. Crying out, she turned her face into his chest, which was damp with sweat. His breathing quickened, along with her heartbeat. Like some cosmic entity had synced them perfectly.

"Oh my God," she said, kissing the thick, salty column of his throat.

He fumbled in his pack, until she heard the crinkling of a foil wrapper. And then felt him put the condom on beside her, could feel his hand against her thigh, rolling it down.

And then he was moving on top of her, and she was spreading her legs open, inviting him in, feeling no shame, no regret.

His biceps shook with the effort of keeping his full weight off her, but she wanted to feel it. Wanted to feel everything.

She traced a delicate line down his rib cage, over his narrow hips and underneath, where she wrapped her fingers around his warm, velvety length. He groaned and twitched once, his muscles tensing. She moved her hand up and down, making him harden even more.

Spreading her legs farther, she guided him toward her. And then he was inside. She arched her back and cried out, unable to help it. He bent his head and found her mouth, muffling the sounds she made. She kissed him back, so consumed with emotion and physical pleasure, that she trembled.

"Maggie," he said against her lips, thrusting deeper, deeper. And it was then that she realized the void she'd been living in these last few months was gradually beginning to change. There was light where there hadn't been before. She could feel it, like sunlight after a long, dark winter, warm on the lids of her eyes.

He thrust again, and she rose to meet him, their lips touching briefly. Outside the tent, a sudden breeze rocked the trees overhead and rustled the grass around its nylon edges. A coyote called again, lonely and distant, and this time the other remained silent.

Maggie brought a leg around the backs of Koda's thighs, unable to get close enough. The climax built inside her, like a wave of electricity, from the core of her belly and radiating outward. It sparked and crackled, touching her in places that had been dead for a long, long time. Her fingers found his shoulders and dug in, holding on.

When she cried out, it wasn't the feeling she would come to remember, so much as the moment itself. As if they were frozen in time. A time that wasn't the present, but not really the past either. It was somewhere in between. A place where there was no such thing as loneliness or loss. It was a place of magic and moonlight.

Where anything was possible.

Chapter Eighteen

Koda lay awake with Maggie sleeping soundly in the crook of his arm. Her face rested against his chest, her silky curls fanned out above them. Every now and then, she would twitch, her eyelashes fluttering against his skin, feeling like the wings of something small and delicate.

He wasn't wearing a watch, but guessed it was around midnight. There was no fog, and the moon, which was just a few nights away from being full, was probably right overhead. He shifted a little, catching the scent of Maggie's hair. She moaned and rolled over. Her pale shoulders rose and fell with the gentle cadence of sleep. An unknown emotion rushed through him, taking him by surprise.

Blinking into the gritty darkness, he wondered if sleeping with Maggie Sullivan had been the smartest thing to do. He'd broken his own rule about not jumping into bed with someone he barely knew. And she wasn't exactly in the best place emotionally, either. Was he going to contribute to that by confusing the ever-loving shit out of her? But even as he thought it, he knew if someone were to put the brakes on here, it was going to have to be Maggie. He was in too deep now.

She moaned again, dreaming, and he pulled the sleeping bag up over her shoulders. There was definitely something about this girl that spoke to him. She was an old soul, something he had been accused of being, too. And when he'd told her she was brave, he meant it. She was one of the gutsiest people he'd ever met, and he'd met quite a few.

He ran a finger down her arm, deep in thought, when a sound from outside made him stop.

Koda held his breath and sat up. *It couldn't have been.* He'd been punchy these last few weeks. Looking for a body, consumed with trying to find a killer, Maggie showing up and turning him inside out. He wasn't normally the kind to spook. But as much as he didn't want to admit it, he'd been spooked several times since she'd come to town.

And then he heard it again. His scalp prickled. The hair on his arms stood on end. A long, eerie howl floated along the midnight air to reach him inside the tent. And this time Maggie stirred.

She opened her eyes. "What was that?"

"Sounds like a wolf," he said, forcing himself to appear relaxed.

She sat up, clutching the sleeping bag to her chest. "But there aren't any wolves around here."

"There aren't *supposed* to be. But that doesn't mean there aren't a few here and there. They've been known to make their way south from Canada."

They sat quiet, waiting. After a long minute, another

howl. It was out of place, enough to send chills all the way down his spine. It reminded him of watching old movies when he'd been little, he and Zane staying up until the wee hours of the morning, scaring each other with their own idiotic legend.

Maggie put a hand on his arm. "Koda…"

"It's okay. Wolves are shy. We should be more worried about bears."

"Great."

Her hair covered one eye and hung in loose corkscrews down her back. Even in the dead of night, out in the middle of nowhere and woken from a sound sleep, she took his breath away.

He leaned over to kiss her shoulder but stopped when another howl cut through the silence.

It was closer this time. Considerably closer.

She scooted next to him and the skin on his neck crawled. Wolves *were* shy, so why was he so jumpy? And what the hell was a wolf doing down here, anyway? Despite what he'd told Maggie, there hadn't been any wolf sightings around here for decades. It didn't make any sense.

Another howl. This time it sounded like it came from the outskirts of the meadow, directly to their left. Maggie sucked in a sharp breath.

"It's okay," he said. "It's all right."

He'd no sooner gotten the words out, than they heard the unmistakable sound of something loping toward the tent.

It was big, whatever it was. The ground seemed to vibrate with it.

Thud, thud, thud.

"Oh my God."

"It's okay." He moved his backpack aside and grabbed the rifle, checking to make sure it was loaded. "Stay here."

She dug her fingers into his arm. "You're not going out there?"

"I'm just going to fire a warning shot. I'm sure that's all it'll take. It's probably just curious, that's all." He pulled on his jeans, then his fleece. Zipping it to his chin, he gave her a quick kiss on the forehead. "I'll be right back."

"Koda." Her eyes were wide and afraid and settled on him with a look of desperation. "Be careful."

He nodded. A few weeks ago, he just wanted her to go back to the city where she'd come from. Now, he knew he'd put himself between her and anything that could hurt her, no matter how dangerous it turned out to be. He'd protect her with his life if it ever came down to that. The knowledge was strangely comforting.

After a long second, he stepped out, holding the rifle close and scanning the moonlit surroundings. The meadow was bathed in silver, frost sparkling over every blade of grass. His breath billowed from his mouth like smoke. He straightened, listening for what they'd heard earlier. But other than his own heartbeat pounding in his ears, there was nothing. No sound, no movement.

Koda walked around the tent, holding the rifle steady. It was impossible to tell what was just beyond the dark line of trees thirty feet to his left. But there was nothing close by. At least not close enough to see. He stopped in his tracks, watching, waiting. *Nothing.*

He stayed there for a good five minutes, his toes numb and his nose running from the cold. He sniffed, beginning to wonder if it had all been a figment of his imagination. Finally satisfied, he headed back to the front of the tent and kneeled to unzip it.

He glanced down at the toe of his boot, the untied laces lying there like miniature snakes. Then froze. Taking a deep breath, he touched the tips of his fingers to a paw print the size of his head.

So much for his imagination.

Maggie sat on the edge of Candi's love seat and tapped her foot, an old anxious habit. Today she was going to meet Bart, Candi's new dog, the alleged vicious protector. Floppy ears and all.

"He's in the back. I'll go get him, just sit tight." Candi had been as excited as a little kid a moment ago, and Maggie grinned back, trying to suppress the nerves that had been gnawing at her since last night.

A paw print. A *huge* paw print. She'd scrambled out of the tent when she'd heard Koda swear under his breath.

"What the…?" Her voice had trailed off. The print was so big, she couldn't believe it had come from an animal, much less, an animal that wasn't even supposed to be living in this part of the United States. They'd looked at each other at the exact moment another howl had pierced the air. Maggie scrambled back in the tent ready to hike out that second. Koda had reasoned with her that they should stay put until first light, but he'd held her for the rest of the night and she was pretty sure he hadn't slept at all.

"Ready?" Candi's sweet singsong voice carried from the

back door.

"Ready!"

Maggie heard the *tick, tick, scratch* of paws that were having a hard time getting a hold on the kitchen linoleum.

"Meet Bart!"

She looked up in just enough time to see a big, brown blob launch itself straight at her.

"Bart, no," Candi cried.

But it was too late. At least seventy-five pounds of slobbery, hairy hound dog was climbing into her lap, licking her ear, under her chin, up her nose. Any place that his long pink tongue could reach.

Maggie laughed, managing to keep his saggy face away from hers, but only by inches. "Oh my God, Bart. You're huge!"

Candi grabbed him by the collar and pulled him off. He looked excitedly from her to Maggie, his long ears swinging back and forth.

Patting his head, Candi smiled sheepishly. "We have a little training still. But I think he's going to be a great dog."

Maggie reached out and scratched behind a velvety ear, getting licked in the process. "He's already a great dog. Aren't you, Bart? Yes, you are. You're a good boy."

Candi sat on the floor and draped her arm around his big, gangly body. He leaned in, and to Maggie's surprise, settled down immediately.

"See?" Candi said. "I think he likes me."

"Of course he does. He knows you're his person."

"You think?"

Maggie smiled at the dog who licked his mistress's face, then collapsed halfway on her lap to expose his chocolaty belly.

"I *know*," she said.

Candi looked up and eyed Maggie. "So. Koda's picking you up here, huh? Going on a date?"

Maggie pulled her knees together. If only Candi knew what had happened between them last night. "Um…yeah. He's taking me to dinner down the mountain."

"I'm glad," Candi said. "I'm glad you two are seeing each other. He's a great guy, Maggie."

Were they seeing each other? Maggie hadn't let herself think that far ahead. But the idea made her happy. "I like him. A lot."

"You light up when he walks in the room, girlfriend. I can tell."

"I do?"

"Yes, you do. And I've never seen him like this with anyone else. Koda doesn't get close easily. Just don't go breaking his heart." She winked. "I like you too much to have to kill you."

Maggie smiled and looked away. The thought that Koda could feel the same way she did made her belly tighten.

"Has he told you anything else about the investigation?" Candi's voice was flat, as if she were afraid of the answer. "Have they gotten any closer to finding the guy who broke in here?"

"I don't think they have anything new. At least not that I know of."

"It's got to be connected, though, right? My bra. Aimee's bra. It's all too weird to be a coincidence, don't you think?

Maggie's chest tightened. She wished she had some answers. Not only for Candi's sake, but for her own as well. But the truth was, whoever was wreaking havoc in Wolfe Creek was very, very good at covering their tracks.

"I do think they're connected," she said. "But so far the police are keeping quiet. They say it's too soon to speculate. There's not enough evidence."

"Bullshit. I think they know more than they're saying."

"Could be. But it's hard to tell for sure."

Candi nodded, stroking Bart's sleek head. "I know it's all classified, but if you hear anything, you'll let me know?"

"Of course I will." Maggie meant it. If anyone deserved to know what was going on, it was Candi.

"I almost forgot." Candi stood, leaving Bart thumping his tail and looking up at her adoringly. "Zane was over last night. Left a shirt to wash. I guess A's machine is on the fritz."

She disappeared into the other room and came back holding a black T-shirt. "He fell in the mud or something. It was covered with it." She handed it over, her face drawn. "He said he was out hiking Pike's Peak. I hate that. It's so dangerous alone. Can you give it back when you see him? I've got to work tonight, and it's one of his favorites."

Uneasy and not knowing why, Maggie stuffed it into her purse. "Sure. Is he okay?"

"As okay as Zane ever is. I worry about him."

"He's lucky to have you."

"I always thought it was the other way around. He walks into a room and everyone notices. He's got this..." She paused, as if looking for the right words. "He's got this life force, you know? I love that."

Maggie wondered how much of that life force was genetic. Koda had the same thing going on, and Maggie was just as taken with it. "I know exactly what you mean."

"We're hopeless," Candi said with a little laugh. "*Hopeless.*"
"Right?"

Bart pricked his ears and stood, looking at the door.

"That'd be Koda," Candi said.

Maggie peeked out the window to see his truck parked at the curb. *Speaking of life force...*

"Let's introduce you two," Candi said to the dog that trotted along after her. "He loves dogs."

Before he could knock, Candi opened the door, holding Bart by the collar.

"Hey you," she said.

Koda stepped in, wearing jeans and a black fleece that matched his hair, and set off the tawny color of his face and neck. *Yum.* He glanced at Maggie and gave her a slow, sexy smile. The same one that had graced his lips last night. They shared a look that sent sparks straight to her core.

"This is Bart," Candi announced, oblivious. "Bart, meet Koda."

Grinning, Koda reached out, but froze at the deep grumble inside Bart's chest. The dog's lips curled away from surprisingly long teeth, and Koda snatched his hand back.

"Bart." Candi jerked on the collar and he sat, but kept his eyes trained on Koda. "I can't believe it. I didn't think he had it in him."

Koda backed up warily. "Looks like he does."

"Maybe he just doesn't like men," Maggie said, standing. Bart immediately turned and wagged his tail. "Some dogs are like that."

"Maybe. Or maybe he just doesn't like me."

Candi leaned forward and sniffed the air. "Did you roll in anything that could have pissed him off? Set off a red flag or something?"

"Yes. I rolled in a patch of Old Spice. Maybe he has a thing against cologne."

"Well, you never know."

"Candi."

"What?"

Rolling his eyes, he touched Maggie's elbow. "Ready?"

"Ready," she said, giving Bart's pointy head a pat.

She didn't know about the dog, but she didn't mind how Koda Wolfe smelled at all.

Chapter Nineteen

Maggie sat across the booth from Koda, sipping her wine and thinking about the T-shirt in her purse. *He must have fallen in the mud.*

Zane had come over to Candi's apartment covered in mud last night, and asked her to wash his clothes. Why?

Koda studied her over the rim of his beer mug. He set it down and licked some foam from his lips. "Want to tell me what you're thinking?"

She smiled. The truth was, as much as she'd been looking forward to this dinner, she was having a hard time concentrating on anything other than her brief visit with Candi. What she'd said about Zane had left her off-kilter.

"Nothing. It's nothing."

Koda frowned and reached out to touch her hand. She watched his fingers wrap around hers. His hands were sexy, the knuckles large and blocky, his fingers long and thick, with intricate blood vessels snaking underneath the dark skin.

"Nice try," he said. "What is it?"

Maggie didn't even know where to start. Tell him about the T-shirt in her purse? Voice her unease about what Candi had said this afternoon? Zane wasn't a suspect, anyway. That was ridiculous... Or was it?

She lowered her head, unable to look at him. She didn't know what to think. She was living in a constant state of confusion. But the fact of the matter was that something about Zane Wolfe bothered her. Something about his posture, his very demeanor. It was more than his cockiness, or unusually good looks. He was mysterious, too. And the reason he was mysterious was because as far as she could tell, no one ever seemed to know where he was or what he was doing.

He could be violent, too. His time in prison proved that. Still, Maggie hadn't wanted to go there for some reason or another. Since she'd met Koda, Candi, and Ara, she felt inexplicably close to their family. She just hadn't been able to think in those terms. Not seriously, anyway. But today... today when Candi had handed over the shirt, a seed was planted in Maggie's brain. It was bitter, suspicious, and desperate. And despite her best efforts otherwise, was growing by the second.

"Maggie," Koda said, squeezing her hand. "Tell me."

"I really don't know how."

He held her gaze, watching, waiting patiently.

When Maggie looked up, it was with some of the stiff resolve that had brought her to this very moment. Didn't she owe it to Aimee to explore every possible scenario? Falling for Koda shouldn't change any of that. She couldn't let it, even if it ended up alienating him. Even if it meant alienating his entire family.

"Remember when you told me I had to be open to every single possibility?"

"I do."

She glanced around, making sure no one could hear them. Only one other couple sat a few tables away, and the waitress puttered near the register. The smell of meat cooking wafted to her and made her sick to her stomach. She swallowed hard, knowing this would be difficult.

And not wanting to hurt this man she could be...no, definitely, was falling for.

"My question is, are you?" she asked.

Very slowly, he removed his hand. Regret hurt her heart, but she had to keep going. Her words would set something in motion, a runaway train of hurt, denial and pain.

"Go on," he said.

Her mouth went dry, and she took a sip of wine.

"Have you considered every single person in Wolfe Creek as a suspect?"

His eyes were dark, wary. "Within reason."

"Koda," Maggie said, wishing there was a comfortable way out of this. Any way out of this. "Don't you think it's strange that no one knows where Zane is half the time?"

"What exactly are you saying, Maggie?"

"I think...you need to consider everyone. No matter how you feel personally."

The waitress came to refill their water, and he waited until she was gone to speak again. When he did, his voice was carefully measured. "You think my own brother could be responsible for what happened to Aimee Styles?"

"I don't know what to think. All I can tell you is that I'm an outsider here, looking in. And I see someone who never seems accounted for. Who stabbed someone—"

"That was self-defense," he snapped.

She composed herself before going on. "Who stabbed someone and spent time in prison. Someone who seems to show up out of the blue injured and dirty. A lot. Why?"

"Because he's still a stupid kid," Koda said, his anger a sudden wall between them. "He gets drunk and does things he wouldn't normally do."

"My point exactly," she said quietly.

He glared at her and picked up his beer, never breaking eye contact. He drained it halfway and set it back down. Hard. "This is unbelievable. What in the world would make you think Zane is capable of murder? *Zane*, of all people?" He shook his head. "You know, maybe this whole thing was a mistake."

She flinched.

"Maybe it wasn't right involving you so much. You're obviously too close to see things clearly."

"Maybe you are, too."

"What I am, is a little pissed off."

"I know you are. I know how this must feel. But you have to look at it from my perspective."

"I don't know what you want me to say. That I'm going to suddenly see my little brother as a killer because you don't like that he bar hops and gets into fights?"

She plowed on, feeling sicker by the second. "Where was he that night?"

Koda's face was stony, his lips almost white. "He was with Candi."

Maggie remembered how intense Candi had looked just a few hours before when talking about Zane. How far away she'd seemed. Maggie's gut twisted. When was this all going to end? "Would Candi lie for him?" she asked, numb, not wanting to believe that.

"Jesus Christ," he said through clenched teeth. She hated how he was looking at her. And hated herself then, too. Hated this whole godforsaken situation. Hated Aimee for being so careless and leaving Maggie to pick up the pieces.

"Why stop there," he said. "Why not suspect me, too?"

She reached for her purse, pulled out the shirt and tossed it on the table. "Candi gave me this today. It's Zane's. He stopped by her place last night. It was covered in mud and he wanted her to wash it. She said he was hiking up at Pike's Peak."

Snatching it, he eyed the faded Led Zeppelin logo on the front. "You think this proves anything?" He laughed bitterly. "All right. You got me. It's proof my brother's a pig and needs to do his own laundry."

Maggie bit her cheek hard and leaned away from him. She wanted to believe in people again. Wanted to trust what they said, what they did. But Koda had no idea how that night had changed her. He hadn't known her before, so he couldn't understand that she was a different person now. A darker person, a more guarded person. That wretched weight had been lifted a little over the last few days, but it hadn't disappeared. Not by a long shot. Until she found out what happened to her friend, it would always haunt her. Always.

"I feel like he's hiding something, Koda. And I'm sorry about that. So sorry. But I can't change how I feel."

"No, you can't."

She stared steadily back, wanting to turn the clock back to a year ago. If she had only kept driving, Aimee would still be alive. And Koda Wolfe would never have been touched by this nightmare.

The waitress brought their food. Neither one spoke. Maggie had long since lost her appetite and Koda looked at his plate as if it were full of cardboard.

"Look," she said quietly. "Let's just be honest, okay? I can't seem to look at anyone without being suspicious, and you can't look at certain people and *be* suspicious. And that's all right. That's okay, because we're talking about your family. I never should have brought this up with you. It was wrong and I'm sorry. I'm sorry I asked you to keep me so involved. It put you in an awful position. We got too close, and now…" She shrugged. "Here we are. I'm sure you're regretting all of it by now. But I can't be sorry, I *won't* be sorry about needing to find out what happened. No matter what it costs personally."

He leaned forward, furious. "You think I regret one second of the time I spent with you, Maggie? Is that what you think?"

"I—"

"You're too wrapped up in yourself to see when someone truly cares about you. And it's not just me. Candi does, too, and she's not a liar. She wouldn't lie about being with Zane."

Maggie's throat ached. "I don't know her that well. It's only been a few weeks."

"Well I do. I do know her that well, and she wouldn't lie. No matter how much she loves him."

"Maybe she doesn't think she's lying. Maybe she thinks he *was* there with her all night. But people fall asleep, Koda."

He placed his hands slowly, methodically in his lap, a gesture that was scarier than if he'd punched the wall instead.

Angry blotches stood out on his bronzed cheeks. She caught her breath, wondering if he really wanted to reach across the table and choke her. *Please, please understand,* she begged silently.

"I don't know what else there is to say," he finally bit out. "If you don't trust me, I don't know how I can help you. Or how any of this can move forward."

It wasn't clear what he meant by "this," but Maggie had a pretty good idea. She wanted to cry, to throw her arms around him and beg him not to leave her alone with all of this. But she was asking the impossible. She was asking that he consider the possibility his brother could have a vicious dark side. A side none of them had seen or even suspected before this. And Koda loved him too much. It was obvious. He'd always been Zane's protector, his buffer against the world. And he wasn't about to stop now.

And neither was Maggie.

"I'm sorry," she whispered.

"Me, too."

"What now?"

"Honestly?" His voice turned to ice. "I just don't know."

A minute passed. Then two, without a single word. Maggie pushed her food around with her fork and snuck a glance in his direction. He was staring at his plate, looking for the most part like he just wanted to get up and leave.

A second later his cell phone rang and he picked it up, glaring at the number. "Wolfe," he said.

Maggie watched him warily.

"McCay. A little. What's up?"

She'd talked to Trooper McCay plenty in the early days. Not so much anymore.

"What?" Koda said, his voice dropping. Something about the tone made her put her fork down. "When?"

A cold feeling, heavy as a lead blanket, settled over her shoulders.

"Okay. Thanks for letting me know. I'm on duty tomorrow. I'll call you in the morning. Later."

He hung up and looked at her.

"What is it?"

Koda appeared to be choosing his words very carefully.

"Another girl disappeared tonight."

Maggie sucked in a breath.

"And this time we have a body."

Chapter Twenty

Maggie moved her clothes from the Laundromat washing machine to the dryer like a robot.

Serial. That's the word Koda had used last night, speaking to her as if she were just another citizen now. Professional, but distant. The events that were taking place in Wolfe Creek had all the earmarks of being connected, he'd said. *It's all speculation at this point, but I think it'll end up being a serial case.*

She'd sat there stunned, unable to believe what he was saying. Another disappearance. And this time the poor girl had been murdered and dumped in a creek two miles down the mountain. She hadn't been from Wolfe Creek, but the fact that her body had been discarded so close was enough for everyone. Including the police. She'd been partially clothed but her bra had been missing.

Their heated discussion not five minutes before had been the proverbial elephant in the room. She wondered about Zane. He couldn't forgive her. And that was that.

"I think you should leave now," Koda had said. "It's getting too dangerous here. I think we can at least agree on that part."

She'd looked him straight in the eye. "I'm not going anywhere. I'm not leaving again."

And that's how they'd left each other last night. He'd been angry, calling her foolish. And maybe she was. But if this was the same person responsible for Aimee's disappearance, he was getting savagely bold. That meant they were getting close. She could feel it. Even if it meant sacrificing her own safety, she had to see this through. She'd come too far to walk away now. They all had.

Her mother was beside herself, of course. Her whole family was. But Maggie had put her head down and dug in.

She'd argued to all of them, including Koda, that if this was a serial murderer in the making, there would be national attention now. And there was some security in that. He wouldn't strike again so soon. And at that, Koda had slammed his hand down on the table last night, rattling the silverware.

"I'm not leaving," she'd said softly.

His anger had actually been a comfort. Because even though he was now decidedly cool, and had made sure to point out that he was only doing his job by wanting to keep her safe just like everyone else, she knew he wouldn't have been as furious with anyone else, either.

Twenty-four hours later, despite everything, despite promising him she'd stay indoors and keep visiting with anyone to a minimum, life plowed on, and she had underwear to wash.

She looked out the window to the misty fog rolling in,

and touched the canister of mace in her pocket. There was still a full hour of daylight left and Ara had known where she was going, when she was due back. Koda was on duty, busy to the point of exhaustion with everything that was happening, but had made a point to check on her earlier.

"I'm fine," she'd said, trying to sound more confident than she felt. "I've got the pepper spray you gave me and I'll be on my toes. Promise."

"I wish you'd go."

"I know. But I can't. I feel like I'd be failing her twice. And I can't live with that."

He nodded, hands in his jacket pockets, his posture aloof, which broke her heart a little. She didn't want him to leave. She wanted to go back to where they'd been the other night. Folded in his arms, feeling his breath on her neck. But that seemed so far away now. Painfully far.

She wondered what it might be like with Koda without this black shadow hovering over them all the time. For just a moment she let herself picture a time, maybe in the not so distant future, where she could walk with him hand in hand down the curious sidewalks of Wolfe Creek. Sidewalks that used to represent a fear of the unknown, the unexplored. But were now possible pathways to another life. One where there was no murderer in their midst, or painful mystery refusing to be solved. For a blessed second, she envisioned the two of them not with dark days ahead, laced with fog and uncertainty like they so often were. But sunny ones, happy ones. Ones with a promise of warmth for them both.

She'd closed her eyes for a second, unable to look at him. It wasn't smart to imagine these things now. It was dangerous to want something that may never be.

"As soon as I'm done here," she'd finally said, "I'll go back to the Inn."

"Call me when you get to your room?"

"I will."

He'd hesitated then, like he wanted to say something more but couldn't find the words. She waited, watching the way his mouth parted slightly, then closed. She'd wanted so badly to stand on her tiptoes and kiss him. To feel his body against hers, so strong and reassuring. But she wasn't entirely sure he wouldn't have pushed her away, and at that moment, it would've killed her.

So she stood there, absolutely still except for her wobbly knees. She held her breath, hoping for a word or a touch, or anything that would make the ache in her throat go away. But whatever he'd been wanting to say or do, he thought better of it and took a step back.

She smiled to hide her disappointment. "So I'll call you soon," she'd said.

And then he was gone, pulling away in his SUV and leaving her alone in the empty Laundromat.

Sitting now in one of the flimsy plastic chairs, she stared at her clothes tumbling in the dryer. She'd finished crying ten minutes ago. Or so she thought. A few leftover tears made their way down her face as if to prove a long-standing point. *You're not as strong as you pretend to be, Maggie,* they seemed to say.

Around and around her clothes went. They fell on top of each other, only to be tossed about again, a virtual tornado of cotton blends and polyester. One of her bras was briefly thrown against the glass before disappearing into the sea of other clothes. She shuddered, wiping her eyes. So the guy had a thing for keeping his victim's bras. *Sick bastard.*

She hugged herself, lost in thought. Behind her, the door opened with a whisper of frigid air and she turned.

Zane Wolfe walked in, looking dark and out of place in the brightly lit room. He wore an old leather jacket and a black wool hat, which was pulled down low, half concealing his eyes. He stopped in the middle of the room, his chilly gaze intent on only her.

Her skin prickled, and she took an involuntary step back.

"Ara said you were down here."

"Yeah." She tried to smile, but couldn't get her lips to fully cooperate. Her hands were sweaty inside her jacket pockets. "I couldn't put off laundry anymore."

"I'm surprised you'd come down here alone. Doesn't seem very smart to me."

Maggie looked beyond him and out the window to the foggy, deserted street. Not a soul out there. She was all alone. Alone with a man who could very well be a serial killer. A man whose expression could only be read as naked aggression.

She wrapped her fingers around the canister in her pocket and felt close to panicking.

"Just so you know," he said. "I never thought it was a good idea for you to be hanging around here. But honestly, I never thought you'd stay this long. Be so persistent."

She shrugged, trying to appear nonchalant.

"You're determined," he said.

"Yes."

"Or just stupid."

"Maybe."

"My brother." His voice was soft. "His judgment seems to be clouded at the moment."

She gripped the pepper spray harder.

"He knows it's not safe for you here. And he knew you'd bring trouble. That's a fucking fact."

"I don't—"

"But now that he's thinking with his dick," Zane continued, "he can't seem to remember that long enough to send you packing."

"I can't leave."

"You should."

"I can't."

They stared at each other for a long moment with the dryer whirring in the background.

Zane smiled, devilishly handsome. Maggie almost forgot she should be afraid of him. *Almost.*

"Well, Maggie Sullivan," he said. "I don't know that you're thinking clearly either."

"I haven't for a while now."

He nodded. The tension between them was unbearable. Maggie's heart slammed against her chest with such intensity, it was making it hard to breathe.

Behind them the door opened. An elderly woman shuffled in holding an armful of clothes. She gave them a toothy smile before making her way to a washing machine on the other side of the room.

Zane watched her pass and then turned his black eyes on Maggie again. The relief she'd felt was short-lived. There was something about those eyes. Something that made her want to cower like a small dog.

"Anyway," he said shifting slightly and appearing to

relax a fraction. "I just thought I'd come by to check on you. Make sure you're okay, since you're hell-bent on staying."

She didn't know what to say to that. *Check on her?* She stared at him, letting the words settle. Her pulse skipped in her wrists. Beside them the dryer whirred, an occasional zipper banging against the hot metal inside. And then, very slowly, what he'd said began to sink in.

He turned to go.

"Zane," she heard herself say.

He stopped and looked over his shoulder. His long hair shone like the hide of a mink.

"Thank you."

His face seemed to soften a little. Or maybe that was just her imagination.

"No problem," he said.

Koda turned on his blinker and merged onto the freeway. He reached for his coffee, spilling some on his hand and letting loose a stream of profanities in the process.

He hated leaving town like this, even for a little while, but there was a possible lead in Splendor Pass that couldn't wait. Patrol was beefed up in Wolfe Creek for the night, and people were being watchful, so that made him feel a little better. But not much.

He thought of Maggie and how she'd looked when he'd left her. So pretty, so full of love and life. The urge to stay had been practically overwhelming. The need to keep her close and safe even more so. But he'd had to remind himself that he had a job to do, and that a lot of people were counting on him. He told himself that with the precautions they were all taking, Maggie would be just fine, and that he'd be back in town in no less than an hour anyway. Still, an uneasy feeling kept nagging at him, making him shift in his seat repeatedly.

Picking up his coffee again, he blew on it before taking a sip. He'd been so angry with her last night that he'd shut off like a switch. Every time he thought about their argument over dinner, he'd block it out, feeling dangerously reactive. But now, making his way down the twists and turns of the mountainside, the nagging feeling continued, until it was like a couple of rough fingernails scratching behind his ear.

He knew Zane wasn't capable of any of this. He knew it. Yet, Maggie's doubt refused to give him any peace. Ever since she'd pulled out that T-shirt and set it on the table, Koda had been feeling off. There were questions where his brother was concerned that he'd been ignoring. Consciously or subconsciously, he'd been pushing them aside, choosing to let his love for Zane override his duty as a deputy. If it had been anyone other than his brother, would he have picked up the lighter from Candi's floor that morning and put it in his pocket? He knew the answer to that, and it made him sick.

The reality was, he felt torn. Torn between loyalty to his baby brother, and the oath he'd taken to protect those who needed him most. And wasn't Maggie at the top of that list? She needed him. Desperately. And he'd turned his back on her because he didn't want to see what was right in front of his face. The fact that Zane had a history of less than stable behavior, and there was evidence now, circumstantial or not, that at least warranted some further attention. If he was Maggie, he'd be demanding it, too.

Koda's duty belt dug into the side of his hip, and he

shifted again trying to get comfortable. All of a sudden it felt too tight, and he wished he could shrug it off. Along with all of the pain and worry and responsibility he'd been carrying around since childhood. He loved Zane. But he'd never understand him. He'd never know exactly what was going on inside his head, and that thought made him shiver despite the warmth of the SUV.

He picked up his cell, and dialed A's number, tapping his finger impatiently on the steering wheel while it rang.

"Hello?"

"A, it's me."

"Is everything okay?"

"It's fine. But I need to talk to Zane. I'd try his phone, but he never has it on him. Is he around?"

"He was, but he left a few minutes ago."

The darkening landscape outside the SUV passed in a foggy blur. The mist grew thick and watery against the windshield and Koda turned on the wipers with a sudden sense of dread.

"Where'd he go?"

"It was strange," Ara said. "He went looking for Maggie."

Maggie opened the door to the dryer and dug out the still-damp clothes. Stuffing them in her laundry bag, she looked out the window as if expecting to see someone standing there looking in. A shadow moved at the corner of her eye and she whipped around, but no one was there. Just like the last time she'd looked thirty seconds ago. She took an even breath. *Great. You're seeing things now, Maggie.*

With trembling hands, she stuffed the last of her clothes in the bag. It was getting dark now with the fog rolling in, and she had no interest in staying there past dark. She'd get back to the Inn, check with Ara, and head upstairs to call Koda. She could hardly wait for the comfort of her little room with the furnace blowing gently in the corner.

Balancing the laundry bag under one arm, she waved to the elderly woman who was engrossed in her needlepoint. Maggie opened the door and walked into the early evening mist, feeling its tiny beads of moisture cling to her face. The town sat quiet, unusually so, and the uneasiness she'd felt in the Laundromat followed her down the sidewalk.

By the time she reached the front steps of the Inn, she hurried to get inside. With one more look behind her, she shut the front door harder than she'd intended.

"Ara?"

The front desk was empty. Maggie walked past and looked around the corner into the dining room, but there was no one there either.

Clutching the bag of clothes, she headed into the parlor where the normally roaring fire was nothing but embers.

The shadows shifted, and she saw a movement to her left. She sucked in a breath and whirled around.

"Hello, Maggie."

Chapter Twenty-One

There, sitting in the corner, was Alan McCay. He was in uniform, elbows on his knees. He smiled slowly. "Did I scare you?"

"Trooper McCay." She let out a breath. "A little. I'm not usually this high-strung."

"I should've known better. Sorry."

"What are you doing here?"

"I've been meaning to come by and talk to you, but something always comes up before I can."

She'd spoken to him on the phone recently, but hadn't seen him in person for months. In the first few weeks after Aimee's disappearance she'd talked to him daily, going over her story again and again. He was instantly likable, with his brotherly manner and brusque speech. Even through her fog of grief, she'd been able to tell he was deeply invested in Aimee's case. But a year had passed, and she'd seen him less and less. He was beyond busy, she knew.

He looked tired now, dark circles under his eyes, deep frown lines at the corners of his mouth.

She hitched the bag of clothes up under her arm and stuck her hip out to keep it from slipping farther. "Oh?"

He glanced around and stood up, imposing in the confines of the little room. She caught the scent of his cologne, which was a little too strong.

"I need to talk to you about Zane," he said quietly.

Her stomach rolled. "Zane?"

"I know he's staying down the hall from you. Koda mentioned it."

She nodded.

"Between you and me, I don't know that Koda is as objective as he should be where his brother is concerned."

She nodded again. She'd thought the same thing, of course. But hearing it from a police officer was unsettling. Zane had stopped by the Laundromat to check on her not ten minutes before, and now she felt conflicted.

"Is he in any kind of trouble?" she asked.

"No. Not yet, anyway."

Maggie's stomach lurched. "Is this about Aimee?"

"Partly, but we can't really talk here."

She moved the heavy bag of clothes to her other arm. They'd made her shirt damp, and she tugged the chilly fabric away from her side. "Okay. Where then?"

"Here, let me." He reached out and took the clothes as if they weighed nothing at all. "I'll carry these up, and then we can grab a cup of coffee. It'll only take a few minutes."

"Thanks. I should let Ara know I'm back, though. She'll worry."

"I already looked for her. She must be out back or

something." He glanced at his watch. "We can call from the car, give her some time to get back?"

"Okay."

"Which room?"

"Upstairs. Third door on the left."

He turned and headed for the staircase. Maggie knew he was probably in a hurry, but looked around again compulsively. The Inn was empty, but the smell of cooking food wafted in from the kitchen. Wherever Ara was, she wasn't too far away.

Climbing the stairs, she brimmed with an odd mixture of comfort and unease. Having Trooper McCay there was definitely a plus, but whatever he had to say about Zane wasn't. She had a feeling she wasn't going to like it. Then what? She thought she'd braced herself for anything, just like she'd promised Koda. But she was beginning to see that the longer she stayed in Wolfe Creek, the harder that was going to be. Maybe downright impossible.

She glanced at the pictures on the wall as she passed, her eyes drawn like always to the wedding photograph, stunning in its black-and-white simplicity. It was beautiful, and for a second Maggie wished she could step back in time. To forget all about the man waiting for her upstairs and whatever questions he needed to ask. She wanted her world to be black and white, too. Simple. No more pain. No more questions.

Pausing for a minute, she gathered her wits. *Here goes.*

Maggie continued up the stairs and down the hallway where Trooper McCay had already disappeared. She caught a trace of his lingering cologne. And something else. It smelled musty up here, damp. She wrinkled her nose. It smelled like the woods. The downy hairs on the back of her neck stiffened.

She dug the key out of her pocket, but when she looked up, the door was already ajar.

She poked her head in to see Trooper McCay dropping the bag of clothes unceremoniously on the floor.

"That's weird," Maggie said. "I swore I locked it."

He stepped around her and pulled the door closed. "You did."

She massaged her arm, which still burned from lugging the bag, and made a mental note to go to the gym more often. "I'm sorry. What?"

"You locked it. I have a key." As if to emphasize his point, he slid the dead bolt across and smiled.

"Oh," Maggie said, confused. "Why would you need a key?"

"I don't need a key. I *want* a key. There's a difference."

Maggie stopped rubbing her arm. They were going to coffee. Why did he just lock the door?

"You seem jumpy, Maggie. It's just me."

She smiled, but took a step back.

"Why'd you come here?" he asked.

"I... Come here?"

"You were safe in Portland." He moved closer, his hands locked behind his back as if interrogating someone. "Well, relatively safe. But back here...you had to know you'd be a sitting duck."

"I needed to find out what happened to Aimee."

"At the risk of getting killed yourself?"

He stared at her, eyes blank, jaw muscles twitching.

"I never thought I'd get killed," she said.

"Well, that was just stupid." He lowered his head just a fraction. "Are you scared, Maggie?"

She tried swallowing, but her tongue was thick and dry. "Why would I be scared?"

He glanced at the dresser. Maggie followed his gaze and saw the top drawer was gaping open like an unanswered question.

"All of your undergarments are gone. I came to visit earlier, but you were doing laundry. So I waited."

It was as if a black curtain were closing in on both sides. The final scene from the horror movie that had lasted an entire year.

So this is how it all ends.

Maggie took a step toward the door, and then another, mildly surprised her legs were still holding her up.

Terror had shown up along with Alan McCay.

"Did you kill Aimee?" she whispered, hardly able to believe she'd said it. The words came from deep inside, from a place that had been slumbering until just now. And all of a sudden, she recognized the smell. The scent from that night in the bathroom. It had lingered there like a dirty secret. *Damp, earthy.* She thought of Candi lying in her hospital bed, bruised and broken. *He smelled earthy,* she'd said. *The bastard tried to take my bra.* The cheap cologne had almost thrown her off. Maggie swallowed and had the urge to throw up.

"I am an officer of the *law,* Miss Sullivan. I've spent hundreds of hours in these woods looking for people. Are you suggesting that I took a human life?" He stepped forward, his movements deliberate and measured.

"You don't help people," she said. "You hunt them."

He laughed.

Maggie felt for her pocket. The mace was still there, hidden away in the folds of her jacket.

"Don't do that," he snapped.

She flinched and dropped her hand to her side.

"Good girl."

"What did you do to her?"

He remained silent, emotionless.

Maggie sagged against the wall, eyeing the gun on his hip. And next to that, a knife in a black sheath.

This isn't happening. She was dreaming in her bed, drenched in sweat. It was a nightmare, the same kind she'd been having for the last twelve months. Only this time, she was having a hard time waking up.

But there he stood. Very real, very cold, and very calculating.

Pulling in a breath, she managed to take another step toward the door.

He shook his head. "She was a fucking mess, that girl. Wild. Don't you think?"

Aimee. Angry tears burned Maggie's throat. *Sweet Aimee.* He was a seasoned detective with years of murder investigations under his belt. Knowing better than anyone how a killer would cover their tracks. Knowing how to cover his own. The realization punched her in the gut, stealing her last bit of composure.

"What are you going to do?" she asked.

"What do you mean?"

"Please don't hurt me."

He looked offended. "I didn't come here to hurt you."

She took another step toward the door.

"I came here to talk to you. Get a feel for how you're

holding up. You've been through such an ordeal."

He moved closer, close enough to touch her.

"Someone had to have seen you here," she said. "They'll know."

"They don't know shit. I'm surprised you don't understand that by now." He paused, reaching out to take a strand of her hair between his fingers. She shrank back and he smiled. "I really was just going to talk to you. But I don't expect you to believe that. Things have a way of changing. Even when you don't intend for things to happen, they do anyway."

She blinked, unable to look at him. His breath was hot against her face, and he took another step, pressing himself against her.

"This is one fucked-up town, Maggie. And not for the reasons you might think."

"You're the one who's fucked-up."

He grinned and put his lips to her ear. "The truth is, I never killed her."

His eyes were so close, she could see the flecks of green and brown in them. "What?"

Tracing the curve of her jaw with his finger, he frowned. "I didn't. But someone else did."

Maggie stood paralyzed, nauseated by his touch. He was playing with her, taking a perverse pleasure in it. "And I'm supposed to ask who?"

"I think you already know."

He dropped his hand and moved it underneath her shirt, seeking her naked skin. Her stomach twisted. She could feel him hard and aroused against her hip.

"Make a sound," he murmured. "And you're dead."

"No. *Please.*"

When he reached for the button on her jeans, she panicked. It was instinct, some long-forgotten female urge to protect herself that made her shove him away with a strength she didn't know she had. His eyes widened in surprise.

And all the while, she saw only Aimee's face, heard only Aimee's voice. *I'll be right back…*

He stumbled back, tripping over the bag of clothes. He reached out to steady himself and caught the lamp in the corner. It fell with him, bouncing off the floor with a hollow *thud.*

"You fucking *bitch.*"

She lunged for the door.

"No you don't," he snarled, grabbing her ankle.

Crying out, she fell against the wall.

He scrambled up and wrapped his fist in her hair. "That was stupid," he said against her cheek. "Really stupid."

She fumbled for the mace. Before she could find it, he twisted her arm behind her back. She tried to scream before he slapped a hand over her mouth. She felt her eyes bug from their sockets. He pushed her onto the floor and straddled her, crushing her with his weight.

His face contorted. He looked like a different person. Beyond the rage, there was insanity. Beyond that, emptiness. And Maggie caught a glimpse of how she might die here. And how he might cover it up, just like the others.

He wrapped his hands around her throat, his thumbs gouging her trachea. Desperate for air, she slapped him, tried to kick, but he didn't budge. He squeezed tighter, his face only inches from hers.

From somewhere in the farthest corner of her mind, she registered footsteps coming down the hall. They were heavy, fast. And then pounding on the door.

"Maggie! *Maggie!*"

Above her, Alan McCay's eyes bulged. A greenish vein stood out in the center of his forehead. He bared his teeth like a dog.

She clawed at him.

"You little bitch," he spit out. "You dirty little whore."

"*Maggie!*"

Someone was ramming the door now. With each blow, the man on top of her squeezed harder. The world began to take on a grayish tinge. The strength in her arms was draining away like liquid. She clutched at his shirt and felt his badge, cold and rigid against her palm.

And then the door exploded inward and bits of frame flew everywhere. A dark shape lunged forward. Zane wrapped his arm around Alan's neck and yanked. The grip on Maggie's throat began to give. Then it was gone, along with the weight on her chest. She coughed and gagged, dragging air into her pinched lungs.

She rolled to her side, fighting for a normal breath. Zane threw Alan to the floor and pinned him there, his lean body straining with the effort. Enraged, Alan twisted around and swung, connecting with Zane's jaw. The sound made Maggie cringe.

Getting to her knees, she fumbled for her pocket. Zane drew his fist back, but Alan jerked to the side. Zane's knuckles cracked on the wood floor with a powerful *thwack* that shook the room.

Maggie crawled forward, gripping the mace like a talisman. She jammed her thumb down, aiming for Alan's face. But at the last second, he grabbed Zane's collar and pulled him down, shielding himself with the other man's body. Zane immediately began to cough and sputter. Coughing himself, Alan used the momentum to give him a brutal shove. Maggie raised the mace again, feeling her own eyes burn as if they'd caught fire. Tears streamed down her face as she pressed the trigger again.

And then, as if in a dream, he drew his gun. She heard footsteps pounding down the hall, Koda calling her name. He seemed so far away.

"This is it," Alan said, moving forward, the breath rattling in his chest. "This is how it ends, little girl. You, then me."

He pressed the gun to her forehead, its steel barrel biting into her skin. She squeezed her eyes shut as thoughts of Aimee flittered across her mind like poisonous butterflies. *I'll be right back…*

She heard Zane cough, heard him rush forward. "*Don't!*"

And then a gunshot, a blast so loud and violent that she collapsed, cradling her head in her hands.

Alan jerked back as if he'd been pushed. Without lowering his gun, he glanced down at the dark circle spreading at his shoulder. It was wet and glistening, soaking his uniform shirt through. She turned to see Koda standing in the doorway. He blocked the light from the hall, his gun in his hands.

"Get the fuck away from her!"

The other man stared back. He seemed to be contemplating the words. For Maggie, time had slowed freakishly. Like they were all moving under water.

"Would you believe I never meant for it to happen?" Alan said, keeping the gun on Maggie, but looking at Koda with vacant eyes. "Would you believe me if I said that?"

"I don't know." Koda was breathing hard, his voice thick

with fury. "I'm sure you didn't mean for it to end like this."

Alan smiled bitterly.

"Drop it now or I swear to God, I'll kill you."

"I always liked you, Koda. You're a smart guy. But not smart enough, apparently."

Koda remained quiet. Sweat beaded at Maggie's temples and dripped down her back. Across the room, Zane stood poised, looking from one man to the other.

"I'm the bad guy here," Alan continued softly. "I get that. But there are other things going on. Right under your *fucking* nose. And you don't even see it. Right under your nose. Too wrapped up in trying to be the Lone Ranger and baby-sitting your goddamn brother to see any of it."

"Drop it, Alan."

The other man smiled, a fine sheen of sweat covering his face. Drops of warm, sticky blood puddled on the floor, and the copper scent made her gag.

"You're right. I didn't want it to end this way. Of course I didn't. You think I'm a fucking idiot? But that's what happens when you have a compulsion, brother. At some point you end up acting on it."

"Alan—"

"Fuck off, Koda."

Maggie could hear the distant wail of sirens. They were coming. More of them. *God, hurry. Please.*

Alan heard it, too. His lips stretched into a grimace. "You have to look *beyond,* my friend. You have to look beyond."

He was raving mad. The hand holding the gun wavered now, and his face twitched abnormally.

"I'm the least of your worries," Alan said. And then, before Maggie knew what happened, he'd turned the gun on himself. He opened his mouth and placed the barrel gently inside.

Maggie shut her eyes.

A shot reverberated through the room. It was too much. She began sinking into blessed darkness.

"Are you hurt, baby? Stay with me." Koda's arms wrapped around her like a blanket. His sweet breath touched her brow, warmed her briefly, but she was so cold. "Don't leave me, Maggie. I love you. I need you to stay with me. I'll take care of—"

She fought the darkness, but it was just too much.

Chapter Twenty-Two

Koda sat in the parlor of the Inn, working on his third cup of coffee. God, he was sick of coffee. Grimacing, he set it down. It was cold and tasted like sludge, but he was anxious to be doing something with his hands other than twisting them.

It was two in the morning, and they had just taken Alan's body away. It had been wrapped in a shroud-like black bag and Koda had to fight being sick as he'd looked on. Maggie and Zane had been questioned extensively in the next room, more to try and gain information about Alan McCay than anything else.

Koda leaned forward and put his head in his hands. In a state of shock for the last few hours, all he'd been able to picture was Alan as he'd been in high school. So likeable, with that shock of brown hair always falling in his eyes. How had this boy who had been loved by so many, who'd had the world at his feet with a successful career and more friends than he'd been able to count, turned out this way?

"I know it's hard to accept, Koda," Ara had said after bringing him the coffee in a chipped white mug. "But he's probably always struggled with this. And you can't blame yourself for not seeing it. None of us did... None of us," she repeated, rubbing his back briefly before leaving him alone in front of the fire.

Now, here he sat. He'd been through the initial debriefing, but was bracing himself for more in the days to come. Much, much more. There would be extensive questions and scrutiny by many. From OSP and other agencies, to the public, about how this man could have held such a trusted position. And for so long.

From what Maggie had said, crying and mostly inconsolable for the first half hour, was that Alan had hinted he'd been responsible for the most recent murder, and probably the attack on Candi as well. But she couldn't shake what he'd said about Aimee.

"He said he didn't do it," she'd sobbed. "He said someone else did."

In the end, she agreed that nothing but time would tell. He was a liar and had been for a good part of his life. He'd deceived his family, his closest friends, his employer. He'd known tonight that the end was near, and was quite possibly planting a seed of doubt, one that would grow over time, long past when he was gone, and would continue to make Maggie's life miserable. Filled with questions and pain. He might have liked the thought of that, Koda had told her. God knew he'd been horribly demented.

They were going to be looking into every single unsolved disappearance in this part of the state, going back to the time Alan had been in junior high. There was no telling what he'd been capable of, even that young. Koda knew that the dusty mysteries surrounding these woods would now be a wide-open book. And who could tell for sure... Maybe they'd solve some, maybe they wouldn't. But knowing what they did now, they had to try.

Koda rubbed the back of his neck and stared into the popping fire. Jim had just stoked it, coming in quiet as a whisper and nodding as he left. It was a silent show of support that Koda was grateful for. The fact that he'd almost lost Maggie tonight was something he still struggled with. It'd only taken a lifetime to find her. A few more weeks to fall in love. And that's what he'd gone and done, wasn't it?

He loved her. How effortlessly that had happened, almost without him realizing it. But when he reached for her earlier and pulled her close, he recognized something else that had grown inside him like a crystal. It was strong. Almost as strong as the love he felt for her.

It was the overpowering fear of losing her. And he instantly understood why she'd refused to let Aimee go all this time. If Maggie had been taken from him like that, he wouldn't have given up either. He would have searched the planet to bring her back, no matter what the cost.

He blinked at the fire, so hot it stung his eyes. The realization that he'd almost lost Zane as well, was enough to make him want to cry. And he hadn't cried since he'd been a kid. He'd come back to the Inn that night with his gun drawn, barreling up the stairs, half thinking it was his own brother he was about to shoot. *Sweet Jesus.*

Now, there was a terrible, lingering guilt for suspecting Zane. But worse, was knowing that his brother could easily have died tonight. The events of the last few weeks were just something he was going to have to give himself time to work through. But he knew without a doubt, that there'd never be another second where he'd be anything less than proud of his wild, reckless little brother.

Sure, he had some secrets.

But when it comes right down to it, don't we all?

Koda rose, his knees cracking as if he were eighty years old. He walked toward the staircase where Ara hovered nearby. He paused to give her a reassuring hug before climbing the stairs to the only place on earth he really wanted to be. By Maggie's side.

Maggie lay still in the crook of Koda's arm, listening to him breathe. His chest rose slightly, and she watched, comforted by the simplicity of it. Rising, then falling again. Over and over. It was a peaceful certainty, something she could count on from one second to the next. His skin was as dark and smooth as an acorn, catching the light from the full moon in the window.

She glanced up, marveling at the frosty glow it cast over the room. The beauty in which it hung there, yet another certainty. No matter what happened on this earth, the moon would keep circling it, keep rising and falling until the end of time.

Maggie sat up slowly, careful not to disturb Koda. He breathed in sharply, then turned into the pillow and relaxed again. She sat looking at him for a long moment. They hadn't made love tonight. He'd come to her and held her while she'd cried, the shock slowly giving way to a dull acceptance that had settled itself over her heart. She knew now she may never know what happened to Aimee. And that was just something she was going to have to live with.

She swung her legs over the side of the bed and walked to the window, tilting her head back to take in the moon. It had been full all those months ago, too. The night that she had made the fateful decision to stop in Wolfe Creek, it had been full and round in the night sky, the fog seeming to give it a wide, respectful berth. It had shown with complete perfection through the evergreens above. *A timber moon.* She hadn't given it much thought then. But now standing here, looking up, she knew she'd never be the same.

She blinked at its loveliness, and before she knew what she was doing, reached for her sweatshirt and boots, and tiptoed out of the room, closing the door behind her. Very soon, it would be dawn. Another day would be born and another night would die, leaving her forever and ever. There would be more moons, yes. But this one, the one that had woken her so gently by peeking into her window, this one would be gone. And all of a sudden, she didn't want to miss another second of beauty.

She padded down the stairs, thinking as she so often did, of that night. Of the moon and the chill of the air.

I can't just leave, she'd said.

You can, the trooper had replied. *And you will. There's nothing you can do tonight. We'll find her, but you have to let us do our job. Can you do that?*

She'd nodded, looking at the weathered sign across the street. The one flanked by the tall pines. Always the pines…

She'd looked back at the trooper, crying, cold, miserable, and her eyes had settled on his name tag. It was a little crooked, as if he'd put it on in afterthought. *McCay,* it had said.

Maggie pulled on her boots now, and shrugged into the sweatshirt. *He'd been there all along.* She imagined him that night, before she'd ever laid eyes on him. Had he been waiting in the shadows? If so, he would have been camouflaged perfectly, disguised as good, but masking a great evil.

She opened the front door and took in a breath, the frigid night air filling up her lungs. Burying her fists inside the sweatshirt pocket, she walked down the steps and into the yard bathed in silver-blue light. Her breath formed clouds of microscopic crystals as she tipped her head back to look at the stars.

Beyond the whitewashed picket fence where the gate hung open, beyond the pile of half-chopped wood, sat the dark expanse of the forest. The trees towered over her, their branches crisscrossing above. Small winged things fluttered in the canopies, and a larger animal, a squirrel maybe, hopped from one branch to the next sending a pinecone tumbling a few feet away.

Maggie stayed very still, concentrating on her breathing, focused on the purity of the moment. The calm that followed was so complete, that she found herself swaying on her feet, a peacefulness seeping into her muscles and bones, the likes of which she hadn't felt for over a year. And then she felt something else. She knew without doubt that she was being watched.

Shivering, Maggie turned, expecting to see Koda coming around the corner, a troubled look on his face, his hair messy from sleep. But there was nothing. Only the darkness and empty expanse of the yard. The delicate frost covering the grass was undisturbed except for her own footsteps.

Beyond the gate, a twig snapped. And then another. Maggie squinted into the line of trees and took a tentative step back. The calm that had covered her just a moment ago took flight and disappeared into the darkness. Another twig broke, followed by the distinctive *crunch* of pine needles underfoot.

"Who's there?" she said, for some reason thinking of Zane, so casually sure of himself. How he'd somehow known she was in danger last night and had come to her room at precisely the right moment. She'd been so scared of him. So sure he was hiding something.

"Who is it?" she repeated, surprised to find herself unafraid now.

The mystical house that cast its shadow over the yard where she stood, seemed to be breathing. Alive. She felt safe inside the confines of the picket fence, as if it was an arm that shielded her from everything that could hurt her. It felt strange, like she was outside her own body, watching herself unfold. The same way she'd felt that night standing at her window, looking down into the yard. When she'd seen the animal crouching at the gate.

Maggie looked up and saw a figure lurking at the edge of the trees. She stiffened, not speaking, knowing she wouldn't be able to if she tried. This was no animal. The distinct, willowy outline belonged to that of a person. A woman, whose halo of hair was visible even if her face was not.

The sensation of floating intensified, until Maggie had to reach out, grounding herself against a nearby stump. Her hand slipped down the damp bark until her fingers found their hold. She stared at the figure in the trees, unable to tell if this was an apparition or something real.

The woman stepped forward, out of the trees and onto the gravel on the other side of the fence. It crunched beneath a pair of soft, leather moccasins. The sound was real; it reverberated in Maggie's ears over and over again. She wore a denim jacket and jeans that hugged her hips and thighs.

Maggie stumbled back, bumping her elbow on the stump. Her funny bone tingled, and she cradled it without thinking.

"Who…?" she began, but her voice trailed off, the words no longer relevant. Her mouth hung open, a fevered pulse building at her temples. She already knew who. Maybe a part of her had known all along. Felt it all along.

"Aimee?"

The name hung in the air, thick and sweet as honey. The woman stepped forward into the porch light. Her hair was long, tangled, but painfully lovely. Dark blond curls as wild as the girl herself. Eyes as black as onyx burned from within a face that was pale and drawn.

Maggie cried out, clutching her chest with both hands, feeling that for an instant, her heart might ram through. The fact that Aimee had always had cornflower-blue eyes didn't matter. Not really.

Standing within a few feet, separated only by a waist-high fence, was her friend. Alive. *Alive.* Aimee's breath formed clouds on the freezing air, her dirty hands twisting together in front of her, Maggie lurched forward with her arms outstretched.

When she got to the gate, Aimee stepped through, just as beautiful as Maggie remembered. But different. She wasn't carrying herself the same. Before she reached her friend, Aimee Marie Styles, missing for exactly one year and eight days, Maggie knew what it was. It was the way she walked. The way she moved with a quiet, dignified grace. The Aimee that Maggie had known, had knocked lamps over on a regular basis. Tripped over bumps on the sidewalk, laughed at her own clumsiness.

This Aimee, the one moving toward her now, was stunning and grave. Taller than she'd remembered. Different. And yet the same, too.

Trembling, Maggie staggered forward and wrapped her arms around her friend. Aimee hugged her back, and they stood there for a minute, crying into each other's hair. Aimee was solid, her arms strong and lean. Her whole body was muscled in a way that nibbled at Maggie's subconscious. She filed it away as yet another difference. Something to be mulled over later when the shock had worn off. Her hair smelled like the woods, her ear warm against Maggie's cheek.

Aimee finally pulled away, looking uneasily toward the house. "Walk with me," she said.

Chapter Twenty-Three

Maggie gaped at her, then wiped her eyes with the sleeve of her sweatshirt. "Yeah. Okay."

Holding the gate open, Aimee waited until Maggie passed, then closed it, dropping the latch soundlessly.

She walked ahead a few feet and Maggie followed, her mind tumbling over itself, a mass of joy, confusion, questions, relief. She found she couldn't hold on to just one emotion, so she stopped trying. She had to trot to keep up with Aimee, who made her way into the trees and shadows on silent feet.

"Where are we going?" she asked, wincing when a branch scraped her thigh.

"Shhhh." Aimee held a finger to her lips and looked back at the house again. Her hair hung in her face. She looked untamed. Uncivilized almost.

"Aimee?"

"Just hold on, Mags."

They walked that way for a few minutes, getting deeper

and deeper inside the woods. The moonlight pierced the trees above, creating an eerie mix of light and shadow. Maggie shivered, watching Aimee's back. Watching her hair swing over angular shoulders and the way she stepped so confidently over the forest floor.

When Aimee finally stopped, it was inside a dense thicket of trees and brush.

Breathing heavily, Maggie looked around. Then rested her gaze on her friend, whom she still couldn't believe was standing there looking back. She shook her head, overwhelmed and a little dizzy.

"Aimee," she began, "what happened?" Her voice wavered and then broke. "Where have you *been?*"

Aimee's face settled into a look of concentration that Maggie remembered well. But those black eyes. Those, Maggie was having a hard time with.

"And what happened to your eyes?"

Aimee touched Maggie's elbow and motioned for her to sit on a fallen log. She did, feeling the dew seep into the seat of her jeans.

"What is it?" Maggie asked, insistent. "You're scaring me."

"I'm not the same person you remember."

Maggie laughed nervously. "No shit." Her smile wilted when Aimee remained serious. "Of course you're not. You've been through hell. It's okay though, because we're going to get you home. We'll get you some help."

"Maggie."

"We'll find you the best doctors."

"Maggie."

"The best therapists—"

"*Maggie.*"

She looked up. "What?"

"I don't want to go back."

Maggie stared up at her, not processing. "What?"

"I don't want to."

"What?" She wasn't sure whether to laugh or cry. *"What?"*

Aimee took a step forward. "I look different, because I am different."

Maggie nodded.

"No." Aimee kneeled down, putting a hand on her knee. "I'm *different,* Maggie."

Maggie looked into her eyes. Surely they were contacts, some kind of disguise. None of this made any sense.

"Listen to me," Aimee said evenly. "It's going to be hard for you. Really hard. But I want you to try and listen to what I'm about to say."

The urge to laugh as if it was all an absurd joke was overwhelming. But the look on Aimee's face remained serious.

"Okay. I'm listening."

"That night, the night we stopped here—"

"I *know* what night it was," Maggie snapped, suddenly angry. Why were they sitting here in the middle of the damn woods, anyway? Why weren't they on the phone to Aimee's parents right this second? She took a shaky breath. "I'm sorry. I'm so sorry. I'm just confused."

Aimee's lips tilted. Small and weary, but familiar. "I know you are. I'm sorry, too. For all of this. But you have to understand, it's never what I wanted. I had no choice."

Maggie twisted her fingers to the point of pain. "Go on," she said. "Please."

"The night we stopped here, when I went to use the bathroom…"

Maggie held her breath.

"He was waiting for me. He was behind the door."

"He?"

"The policeman. The trooper."

"Aimee."

"He wasn't in uniform. He wore a mask. He grabbed me from behind and put an arm around my neck." She seemed far away when she said this, her voice barely audible. "He was so strong. Said if I made a sound he'd kill me. He dragged me through the window and into the woods."

Maggie touched her own throat, remembering how Alan's hands had felt wrapped around it. So that was what had happened that night. Her stomach roiled, and she felt like she would be sick.

"When he got me far enough in, he started groping me." Aimee's face was pained, but composed. Maggie had the distinct feeling this was for her benefit. "He tried to take my bra. Of course. Sick fuck."

And there was a glimpse of her old friend. The dry humor that Maggie had loved so much.

"He was going to kill me. I knew it. It's strange, you know? All those things you hear, about what to do in a situation like that. I couldn't remember any of them. I couldn't remember shit. All I kept thinking was, *This is how I'm going to die.*"

"How'd you get free?"

Aimee looked away, seeming to hear something in the forest Maggie couldn't. "I didn't. Not on my own."

Maggie's blood chilled.

"Someone helped me."

"Who?"

When Aimee looked back, her eyes seemed infinite inside her delicate face. "Jim."

"Jim…Jim…the *caretaker?*"

Aimee nodded.

"What?" Maggie was having trouble breathing. "How? Why? Why didn't he *say* anything?"

"Because. He has a secret, Maggie."

"A secret."

"Remember when I told you that you needed to hear me out? You're going to have to listen very carefully, okay?"

Maggie dug her fingers into the log where she sat, jamming bits of bark underneath her nails. A piece of bark broke off. The moss was slick and soft against her skin, and she held on for a minute, rubbing her thumb back and forth over it.

Aimee reached over and stilled Maggie's fingers, the touch familiar. She shoved the bark in her pocket, finding comfort in its cool, earthy texture.

"Okay. Sure. I'm listening."

"Jim isn't what he seems."

"He's not a caretaker?"

Aimee smiled at this, but it was Maggie's turn to be serious. She was beyond confused. All of this was getting weirder by the second.

"He's Koda and Zane's uncle from their father's side. His name is James Bastien Wolfe. No one but Ara knows that. Until now."

Maggie considered this, felt a strange prickling sensation and then understood why. "Koda and Zane. Ara," she said. "You know them?"

Aimee shook her head. "I know *of* them. But I don't

know them. Not like you."

"Their uncle." Maggie sampled the words on her tongue. "Why wouldn't he tell them?"

"Because. The fewer people who know about him, the better."

Suddenly Maggie didn't want to hear any more. It was all getting too bizarre.

Aimee's strange dark gaze settled on hers. "Jim didn't so much see what was happening to me, as he sensed it."

Maggie waited, silent.

"He sensed it because the Wolfe men...they're special."

Above them an owl hooted. The sound sent shivers up Maggie's back. What she really wanted to do was get up and walk away before Aimee spoke again. But she forced herself to sit still. Because she loved her and couldn't bear to leave her again. No matter how freaky she sounded.

"You know about the legend." Aimee said.

"The legend," Maggie repeated, as if it would start to make more sense. Her entire body felt coiled, ready to spring.

"You know about the lupus, the family tragedies."

"Yes."

"There's no lupus."

"Thank God," Maggie said.

"It was just an explanation."

"For?"

"Early deaths and disappearances. Because the tragedy part *is* true."

Maggie immediately thought of Koda's father who'd died so young, and her head throbbed. She fixed Aimee with a wobbly stare. "So they have bad luck?" She wanted it to be that simple, wanted Aimee to stop right there and not say anything more. But a tiny spot of clarity began to reveal itself inside her brain.

"You could say that. Among other things."

"What? Just tell me." She took in Aimee's features, beautiful, apprehensive. Whatever it was, her friend worried about saying it out loud. Maggie was worried, too. And for whatever reason, all she could think of was that spine-tingling howl she'd heard that night with Koda. *There are no wolves around here,* he'd said.

Aimee sat back, the heels of her moccasins sinking into the bed of pine needles. "Well, here's the thing. The legend... the part about werewolves..." She took a long breath, blowing it out slowly. "That part is true."

Maggie laughed. It was high pitched and shrill. Almost loony. She looked at Aimee and wiped a tear from her eye. "Excuse me?"

"It's true, Maggie."

"You can't be serious."

"I'm very serious."

"Aimee —"

"Mags." Aimee cut her off. "If you're being honest with yourself, deep down, I think you probably already knew."

Maggie laughed again. "That's ridiculous. I never believed any of that crap. And what's really hard to swallow, is that you do. Why, I don't know. The only thing I can think of is that you've been traumatized."

"That's true. I've been through something horrible. But I'm not crazy."

"How do you expect me to believe this? God knows I love you. I'm so thankful, and...and..." She was having trouble getting the words out. None of them fit. None of them were strong enough or encompassed all of what she was feeling. "I'd do *anything* for you. You're my family. But…"

"But what?"

Maggie rocked back and forth, hugging herself.

"If you really love me, you'll believe what I'm saying. It's imperative that you do, Maggie."

Aimee stood. She was so tall now, so different. Her eyes, her build. Things that Maggie had questioned in the back of her mind, but knew she'd be able to explain away later. Now, she wasn't so sure. She wasn't sure of anything anymore. Coming back to Wolfe Creek had turned her world upside down in more ways than one. Everything that she believed to be true about her life had changed the second Aimee had walked back into it.

"This is a magical place," Aimee said. "There's more going on here than an outsider could ever guess. I think it's always been this way. Magic exists, but most people are just too busy to notice."

Maggie remained quiet. *Magic.*

"I think maybe we stopped here for a reason," Aimee said. "I think I went into that bathroom at exactly the moment I did, because I was meant to."

"You never believed in fate before."

Aimee shook her head, her long, tangled hair moving against her cheeks. "No, I didn't. But I do now."

"So what happened? When Jim…appeared?" Maggie couldn't bring herself to believe any of this, but there was a strange compulsion driving her to ask.

"I'm going to tell you, but I need you to stay calm, okay?"

"I will."

Aimee narrowed her eyes. They sparkled even in the

darkness. *"Really* calm."

A tranquility settled over Maggie's shoulders. She nodded. *Those eyes.*

"Jim saved my life that night. The trooper ended up getting away, but I was caught in the middle."

Goose bumps prickled Maggie's legs.

"I was accidentally bitten."

An owl hooted again. Something scampered off to the left, rustling the bed of dry leaves. Maggie remained still, soaking in the words. Bitten. *Bitten.* What the fuck did that mean? Did she have rabies?

Aimee watched, intent. "Say something."

"I don't know what to say. Are you telling me that Jim bit you?"

"Yes."

"Are you telling me that you were bitten by a...*werewolf*?"

Nodding slowly, Aimee stepped forward.

"So...so you're saying you're a werewolf." The words fell from her mouth like boulders.

Aimee leaned down until she was within just a few inches. Maggie could actually feel the heat coming off her skin. Could feel the sweetness of her breath against her forehead.

"Yes," Aimee whispered.

This time Maggie didn't laugh. She looked at her friend, the girl whom she'd grown up with, shared so many secrets with. The girl she thought of as her sister. And felt only pain.

"Why are you doing this?" she asked.

Aimee bent to one knee, her expression mirroring Maggie's. "There was no way around it. You had to know."

"I can't believe this, Aimee. I'm so sorry, but I just can't."

Aimee didn't answer. Instead, she reached out and

wrapped her long, graceful fingers around Maggie's wrist.

"Ouch. You're hurting me."

Aimee's midnight eyes widened, their shape actually changing, growing.

"*Ouch*," Maggie said, trying to pull away. But the hand that held her wouldn't allow it. It was like a steel trap. Her heart drummed in response, and she wanted to run.

Before Maggie knew what was happening, Aimee clamped her other hand over her mouth. She struggled, too caught up in a rush of panic to understand.

An electricity pulsed beneath Aimee's hot, dry skin. It was salty against Maggie's lips and smelled like meadow grass. She tried to scream, but couldn't.

"It's okay," Aimee said. "I'd never hurt you, Maggie. I love you. Don't you see? I've been with you this whole time."

Maggie shut her eyes. Sharp, vivid memories came at her one after the other. They were relentless. Hitting the dog on the freeway, the howl rolling over the meadow where she'd slept with Koda, the night she saw the animal crouching by the gate. All of them assaulted her at once. *Aimee. It had been Aimee all along.*

And when she looked back, her friend's eyes were no longer black.

They were a bright, lustrous gold.

Chapter Twenty-Four

Maggie stopped struggling. Her body stilled as if she'd been shot full of a tranquilizer. Even her heartbeat slowed, filling her with a sense of calm that was probably just pure and absolute exhaustion.

Hesitantly, Aimee removed her hand from Maggie's mouth. Somewhere in the darkness a lone dog barked. And farther away, dulled by distance and landscape, was the sound of the freeway where the occasional log truck barreled down the mountain.

"What…?" Maggie couldn't finish. She didn't know how.

Aimee's burnished gaze was almost serene. "It's true," she said quietly.

True. *True.* It couldn't be. Couldn't possibly be. Yet, the light reflected in Aimee's animal eyes confirmed what she'd been feeling all along.

All this time, she'd been watched. She hadn't imagined it. *It was true.*

Maggie opened her mouth to speak, but Aimee stopped her.

"Don't. It's going to take some time, Mags."

"But why?" she choked out. "Why are you telling me now, after all this time?"

"You were on the verge of finding out, anyway. You weren't supposed to. But I know you, and you would have put it together eventually. And I wanted to be the one to tell you."

"What about Koda? Is he…?" Maggie thought of the man she'd fallen so helplessly for. She pictured his eyes, black like Zane's. Black as the night she was sitting in now. How could she ever wrap her mind around this?

"He doesn't know."

"How could he *not?*"

"It doesn't happen right away. It might never happen for him. But it did for his father. It could for his boys."

"And Zane?"

Aimee wet her lips. "It's too early to tell, but Jim thinks yes. Maybe for Zane."

It took every bit of strength Maggie had not to cry out. The curse really existed. Magic surrounded Wolfe Creek, and was tangible in the form of the men who bore the same name. They carried it with them without even knowing.

"Don't be afraid, Mags," Aimee said, touching the spot on Maggie's wrist that was faintly purple now. "Something terrible happened a long, long time ago. It's changed so many lives. But the tragedy stops there." Her face turned up, stunning in the moonlight that settled over it. "Things happen in life. You can choose to be beaten by them, or you can choose to see the beauty and peace that's almost always there if you look hard enough. I *choose* to live my days as something good. Something worthy."

And with those words, there was finally a moment of understanding that Maggie could grasp. Whatever Aimee was now, she would never hurt her, Maggie knew that. And neither would Jim. They wouldn't even hurt Alan, as dangerous and deadly as he'd been. Aimee carried with her a realm that might take a lifetime to figure out. But she also carried her humanity as well. Maggie could see it in her friend's expression. That part hadn't changed. If anything, it had grown stronger.

"I'm grateful," Maggie whispered.

Aimee's sun-colored eyes were glassy. "Me, too. But there's no perfect ending to this story. We can only take each page as it's read to us."

Maggie put her hand on Aimee's, feeling the power there, the heat.

"I'm not sorry about what's happened to me," Aimee said. "It's taken a long time, and there are moments when I still struggle with it. But I believe this is a gift. I really do."

Maggie considered this. "Will you ever go home again? Your parents, Aimee. They're heartbroken."

"I don't know." Aimee looked away. "It's complicated. I miss them so much. Maybe someday. But for now I need to be here. These woods are where I'm most comfortable. And there are others. Living in society is possible, but for me it's harder. I just need more time."

"So you're going to stay dead." Maggie felt the certainty of the words before they'd even formed on her lips.

"For now, yes. Until I can think of something better, yes. It's the only way."

"What about me? What do I do now?" She felt like she was being let out of a car on the side of a deserted road. She didn't know whether to turn left or right. If she wasn't the girl looking for Aimee, then who was she?

Aimee looked up. "You go home. Or you stay put. You do what you feel is right in your heart. But I think your heart is what led you back to this place." She smiled then. "And maybe it wasn't just to find me. There's love for you here, Maggie. I feel it."

The great expanse of sky above was turning a gritty blue, the moon disappearing behind the gray-velvet mountaintops. The stars were fading, until soon they'd be only a memory of another night gone.

"It's going to be light soon," Aimee said, helping Maggie up. She wrapped a steady arm around her shoulders and pulled her close. It felt like coming home. "Let's get you back."

"Maggie."

A bright orange light shone through her closed lids. Beneath her cheek, a pillow that smelled like fabric softener.

"Maggie."

Rough hands nudged her gently. And then breath on her temple, stubble against her skin.

She lay perfectly still, feeling as if she were moving inside the feathered walls of a dream. She opened one eye, just a slit, but enough to let a golden shaft of sunlight in.

"It's eight," Koda said, kissing her again. "I know I should have let you sleep, but I'm going to be on duty for the next few days and won't be able to see you much. I was hoping you'd want to grab a bite before I go in."

Maggie rolled onto her back. It felt like she'd been asleep

for days. Or weeks, even. Her head throbbed insistently. *Aimee, Aimee, Aimee,* it seemed to say. She opened her eyes to see Koda swimming there.

"Hey, lassie."

He looked so handsome in his uniform, his black hair shining in the morning light. She reached for him and his face softened.

He leaned down and she wrapped her arms around his neck, beginning to cry.

"Hey, hey, *hey,*" he said, pulling back. "What is it?"

She rubbed her eyes, embarrassed. He'd caught her at such a raw moment, with the dream still painfully fresh.

"It's nothing."

"What?" He looked so concerned that her heart squeezed. All of a sudden, she wanted to see him smile. More than anything. They'd all had enough worry to last a lifetime.

"I just had the most bizarre dream."

"About?"

She turned toward the window and squinted at the sunlight coming through the glass. The lovely prisms of yellow, orange, and red. "About Aimee." She looked back at Koda on the verge of saying more, but stopping short. The feeling of seeing Aimee again was still so real, that she wanted to keep it to herself a while longer.

"I'm sorry, Maggie. For everything."

"Don't be." She put a hand on his thigh. "Really. Don't be. It all happened the way it was supposed to, I think. And as crazy as it probably sounds, deep down, I feel like wherever Aimee is, she's okay. Does that make sense?"

His expression was bittersweet. "Perfect."

Her mouth tipped at the memory of the dream, of her

friend's sweet voice. *You can choose to see the beauty and peace...if you look hard enough.* She was so lucky to have known Aimee. For meeting her when they'd been little girls, for growing up together and creating a patchwork quilt of memories, joyful and grim, clear and vague, near and far. They would always be a part of who she was. And so would Aimee.

She held Koda's hand, reluctant to let go. "I'll get dressed and be right down."

"Okay," he said, tugging on a curl. His dark eyes locked with hers, and he leaned down to kiss her for a long, wonderful minute. She felt his tenderness there. Love. She could feel it. *That's how it should be.* Life went on.

She washed her face, dressed quickly, and came down the stairs to where Koda was waiting at the front door. Ara was there, too. When she saw Maggie, she pulled her into a hug.

"I'm glad you're here," she said simply. Maggie gazed into the other woman's face and saw for the first time how lovely her eyes were. A deep blue gray that seemed to hide nothing. "I hope you find what you're looking for." Winking, she turned and disappeared into the kitchen where the scent of something baking waited.

Maggie stared after her. *Your heart is what led you back to this place,* Aimee had said. *And maybe it wasn't just to find me.*

Koda took her hand and led her out the front door. She squeezed his fingers, knowing now that he had opened his guarded heart enough to let her in. *Really* let her in. And that would never stop thrilling her. "Hope you don't mind if Zane and Candi join us," he said. "They invited themselves."

"I'd love that."

Together they stepped down to the walkway. The fall morning was crisp and impossibly bright. The sound of chopping wood reverberated through the air. Maggie turned to see Jim at the side of the house, tall and imposing, raising his ax and bringing it down to split a fat piece of wood. He wore an old denim coat and had a pipe in his mouth. She caught a trace of its pleasant smokiness and for some reason was comforted by it.

Maggie's stomach rumbled. Suddenly she couldn't wait for breakfast. It felt like she hadn't eaten in ages.

A breeze moved the pine boughs above, making them sway and shiver in the sunlight. A stray curl blew across her face and she tilted her head just in time to see something small and dark flapping on the hinge of the gate. She brushed her hair away and stopped, curious.

Koda was already on the sidewalk, whistling something unrecognizable, hands deep inside his jacket pockets. He turned. "Coming?"

"Yeah," she said. "I'll be right there."

"Just so you know, Zane's a pig. He'll eat everything before we get there."

She grinned. Tucking her chin inside her collar, she crossed the lawn toward the gate. Overhead, a hawk cried. Maggie looked up and shielded her eyes, watching it dip and sway on the wind.

The gate creaked and blew open a little, then hit the post again with a *bang*. She looked down. There on the hinge, was what had caught her eye. Hesitant, she reached out and took a small tuft of fur between her fingers. It was soft and textured, the tips of the hair, a deep charcoal black. Her heart drummed a steady rhythm as she brought it to her cheek. It smelled like meadow grass.

Behind her, the chopping came to a stop, leaving the air

naked and quiet. The house cast a long shadow, as if reaching out to touch her on the shoulder.

She turned to see Jim watching her, the ax in his hand, the pipe between his teeth. Before she could say anything, he gave her a knowing smile and turned away.

Maggie stood looking toward the little town that was tucked so perfectly away inside these vast, sprawling woods. The rooftops of the old houses were laced with frost and sparkled underneath the morning sun.

Her hands were chilly at her sides. Shivering, she shoved them in her pockets and jabbed her finger on something sharp. Pulling it out, she saw a piece of moss-covered bark.

Magic? The word was plump with meaning. She wrapped her fingers around the tuft of fur and placed it lovingly, gently into her breast pocket. *Just maybe.*

She walked toward Koda, wanting to stay, but not knowing if he wanted the same. "I guess I need to pack when I get back from breakfast."

He stopped and faced her. "Why?"

"We know what happened to Aimee now."

He watched her for a moment, his eyes mirroring the longing she felt. The desire. But was that enough?

"Don't go," he said softly.

"What?"

"I want you to stay."

She considered this. Needed so much to believe it, but all she could think of was how much he'd tried to get her to leave before. "Do you really want me to stay, Koda?"

"I do." He stepped closer. "Honestly, I can't see my life here without you in it. Don't you know I've been waiting for you? I didn't understand that before. But I do now."

He slowly leaned forward and pressed his lips to hers. The kiss made her dizzy, and when he leaned back, she touched her tingling mouth, savoring the feeling.

She grinned, so full of joy she thought she might break from it. It had been so long since she'd felt *joy*. Pure and sweet, and consuming her completely. "Aren't you afraid someone will see you kissing an outsider?"

"You're no outsider now, lassie. You're mine. If you'll have me."

His… One little word that meant everything.

"Okay," she said, her throat aching. "I'll stay."

He held his hand out and she took it, stepping close. Together, they walked along the curious, cracked sidewalk that led into Wolfe Creek, a town so often cloaked in fog. But it wasn't today. At that moment Maggie realized a simple truth. She knew that this sidewalk could lead to so much more. It was a pathway toward a brand-new life. A new love.

She hadn't been able to trust anyone for so long. She'd been scared of the unknown, of the mysterious and unproven. But holding onto Koda now, she knew she'd let him lead her anywhere. Down this sidewalk and beyond. Because she trusted him with her life. Her healing heart. And even more precious, her future.

"By the way," he said, smiling down at her. "What'd you find?"

The smile looked perfect on him. Magical, as a matter of fact. She smiled back, feeling the sunshine warm on her shoulders.

"Exactly what I was looking for," she said.

THE END

Acknowledgments

I wouldn't be able to do this job that I love so much without the constant, unwavering support of my family. Especially my husband who has been there for every bend in the road. Love you, babe.

Thank you to my wonderful and diverse group of friends, some of whom are writers, some of whom are readers, and some of whom just like to knock back a glass of wine with me every now and then. You know who you are and you make my world a brighter place.

To the people who run the real historical inn that inspired this story, thank you for your support and encouragement, and for opening your doors to history geeks like me.

And finally, thank you to my editors, Candace Havens and Allison Collins for all of your hard work, dedication, and knowledge of the written word. I'll be forever grateful.

About the Author

For Kaylie Newell, writing ranks right up there with the things she loves most in life—falling somewhere behind her family, but ahead of Bradley Cooper (which says a lot). She fell in lust with the romance genre when she was about thirteen and began sneaking her mother's paperbacks from the bedside table. After acne, college, marriage and kids, she decided to take a crack at writing one herself. Turned out to be the best adventure she's ever taken. When she's not dreaming up her next book, she's usually eating chocolate or walking the family mutt. In that order.